FUTURELAND

BATTLE FOR THE PARK

ILLUSTRATED BY **Khadijah Khatib**

FUTURELAND

BATTLE FOR THE PARK

= BOOK ONE =

WRITTEN BY

H.D. HUNTER

WITHDRAWN

RANDOM HOUSE 🏠 NEW YORK

Text and art copyright © 2022 by Cake Creative

All rights reserved. Published in the United States by Random House Children's Books, a division of Penguin Random House LLC, New York.

Random House and the colophon are registered trademarks of Penguin Random House LLC.

Visit us on the Web! rhcbooks.com

Educators and librarians, for a variety of teaching tools, visit us at RHTeachersLibrarians.com

In association with

Library of Congress Cataloging-in-Publication Data is available upon request.
ISBN 978-0-593-47942-1 (trade)—ISBN 978-0-593-47944-5 (lib. bdg.)—
ISBN 978-0-593-47943-8 (ebook)

Printed in the United States of America
10 9 8 7 6 5 4 3 2 1
First Edition

For Charli

For "The List"

And for Rob, who was also
once the new kid in Atlanta

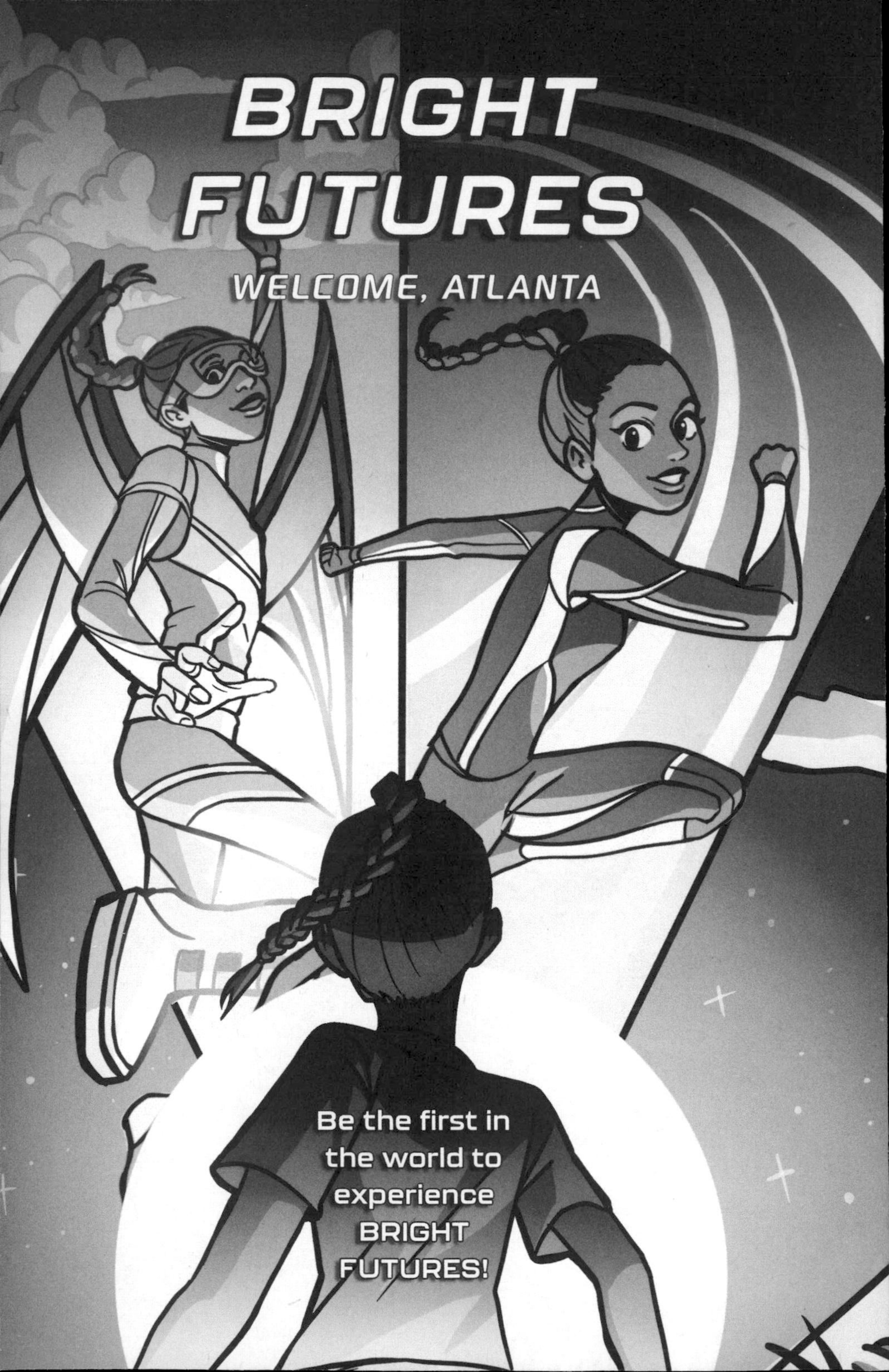
BRIGHT FUTURES
WELCOME, ATLANTA
Be the first in the world to experience BRIGHT FUTURES!

An exclusive new Futureland exhibit

Be sure to bring your dreams, big and small, along with you!

INTERVIEW OUTPUT REPORT 0001

Date: 08-29-2048

Location: Undetermined

Interviewer: Unlogged

Subject: Undefined

INTERVIEWER: Are you awake?

SUBJECT: I do not require sleep. I am currently functioning at full capacity.

INTERVIEWER: Right. Let's get to it, then. What do you know about Futureland?

SUBJECT: Futureland is the world's most popular and innovative theme park. The entire park flies from city to city, making it accessible to guests around the globe. Most recent stops include Tokyo, London, and Chicago. The creators of Futureland, Stacy and J. B. Walker, collaborated to design and manage the park—the first-ever experience of its kind. The park currently consists of ten worlds—

INTERVIEWER: Stop. What do you *really* know about Futureland?

SUBJECT: I'm sorry, I don't understand.

INTERVIEWER: What is the secret to the Walker technology? How did they create everything?

SUBJECT: I'm sorry, I don't understand.

INTERVIEWER: [*microphone registered silence*]

SUBJECT: I'm sensing tension. Is there anything I can do to make your experience better?

INTERVIEWER: We're running out of time.

SUBJECT: Thank you for coming. We hope to see you again.

INTERVIEWER: Wait—a few final questions. Do you know where you are?

SUBJECT: Internal Global Positioning mechanism status: deactivated.

INTERVIEWER: Good. And do you have a name?

SUBJECT: Yes. We are all given names.

INTERVIEWER: Disgusting. Well, what is it?

SUBJECT: My name is [*transmission corrupted*].

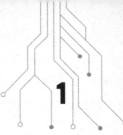

1

THE BUGGED-OUT REV

Sunday, August 30, 2048
7:23 a.m.

Look, you'd probably think I was the luckiest kid in the world . . . because I live on top of it.

No, seriously.

Literally.

Well . . . more like above it, if I'm being *precise*—vocabulary word! (My teacher, Madam Bonnier, would be proud.) I'm growing up in the coolest, most famous theme park. Ever. Like, *for real* for real.

Yeah, yeah. That one. Only one above the rest.

FUTURELAND.

Seen the holograms of my mom and dad on your news tablets? Maybe they even mentioned me—their only child. Bet you wondered what life was like growing up in a roaming theme park. You probably called us the luckiest family in the world.

Maybe.

Most kids would think having a permanent ticket to Futureland would be the best thing ever. A regular kid might be so gassed up, they'd turn into an insomniac. You know, the people who stay up all night guzzling down coffee—which Dad says stunts your growth—and wandering the park destinies until the sun comes up. Or they'd get heads so big, they couldn't even strap into the Jet-Blur and fly around to each exhibit.

To me . . . Futureland was just home. And on most days, I loved it.

But this was *not* one of those days.

"Good morning, Cameron Walker," Dooley chirped, bursting into my room and leaning over my bed. Her unblinking eyes scanned me, the irises turning from hazel to neon orange.

I covered my head with a pillow. "I'm still sleeping."

"You are verbalizing, so you must not still be sleeping, and your mother asked me to wake you."

I let out a big snore and covered my face with my top blanket. It was Scooby-Doo themed. My favorite show on my favorite blanket, of course. "Ugh. It's too early."

Dooley yanked the covers back. "Actually, it's seven-twenty-five a.m. You're five minutes and three-point-two-five seconds late to meet your mother, though I see that you're in need of at least another hour of sleep, based on your oxygen levels and brain waves."

"Yeah, yeah, good morning to you, too." I opened one eye, spotting her two perfectly round afro-puffs.

I scowled.

She smiled wide. Our grins were identical, our skin was the same shade of bronze brown, and our faces had the same tiny, star-shaped birthmark below our left eyes. Mom designed her like that so most people would think we were family. So I wouldn't be lonely. Sometimes I'd forget Dooley was even a rev. She fooled just about everyone. People called Mom's androids the best ever made.

"You are now seven minutes late to meet your mother."

"Fine! *Fine!*" I rolled out of bed, brushed my teeth, and pulled on an old Futureland T-shirt. I flipped through a few pages of a Watson and Holmes graphic novel while I brushed. Probably reading more than I was brushing, honestly. I like the new version set in Harlem, New York. "Dooley! Where's Mom?" I called out.

"Elevator." Dooley practically yanked me through the condo. Only tiny colorful lights marked the path, the windows blacked out by the auto-shades. "Here, take these," Dooley said as we rushed, handing me a pair of Future-vision goggles—the special, high-tech eyewear that helped us navigate Futureland and see all its wonders.

"Are these new?" I asked.

"Somewhat." Dooley grinned mischievously, whispering as we got closer to my mom. "I've been tinkering with them."

"Hey, Cam-Cam. Missed ya." Mom squeezed me tight and kissed my forehead, and I secretly wiped it off. "Took you long enough."

"What are we even doing? I was still sleeping."

"You know the deal. . . . The Walkers walk the walk, and that means we're up and at 'em," she said, placing her palm flat on the wall beside the elevator doors. They slid open silently, and a soft green light welcomed us in. "Plus, I need your kid brain."

There was no way out of this. . . . When Dr. Stacy Walker made up her mind about something, nothing could change it.

"So where are we going?"

"Uncle Trey called. Said there was a problem with one of the gorilla-revs. Malfunction. Something he couldn't fix. He's across the park dealing with a digi-water leak in the Future Ring. We're too close to opening day for anything to go haywire. Told him my right-hand man and I will handle it."

"That's Dad."

"He's the left hand," she said with a smile.

"Wait, there's something Uncle Trey couldn't fix?" I asked, shocked. My uncle is, like, King of the Handymen. He could probably even reignite the sun if its light ever went out.

Mom raised her eyebrows and nodded. "I know, I know, I said the same thing." She touched my hair, then the beehive of locs she'd been growing ever since I was born. "Trying to be like me, kid? Growing out nicely."

"I'll catch up." I peeped the new crop of twists sprouting from the top of my head in the elevator reflection and smiled.

"Destination?" the elevator asked.

"Walker Family Jet-Blur Hub," Mom replied before turning to me. "You ready?"

"Always." Even though I complained sometimes, I still loved exploring the park with her and helping with the revs and new tech. I was always the first to try out all-new exhibits or role-play a guest in Dad's latest story lines. They needed kid approval. They needed *my* expertise.

"Good. It's important you know the ins and outs,"

Mom said, like she always did. I noticed her smile from a side glance. She was so proud. I felt a little guilty that I'd rather have been still snoozing in bed—or reading one of my crime books.

The elevator shot straight up. Silvery walls turned to glass as it made its way to our private park entrance: a massive train terminal with floor-to-ceiling windows.

We stepped out. Wall-o-gram billboards twinkled and flickered, filling with photos from different Futureland eras.

"Good morning, Walkers," said one of the guard-revs standing at the entrance. His uniform shone bright, and the Futureland pin on his jacket glowed.

Mom nodded at him.

"Please step on a Jet-pad and prepare for travel," he said.

We each jumped on an outlined box on the floor: the foot sensors that called the Jet-Blur to take us to the park destinations.

This might be my favorite thing my parents made. I pressed my face against the glass, watching as the park's transportation system burst into view: a high-speed travel pod with room for three. When the park was open, there'd be hundreds of these in the air like cool black marbles threaded with gold, each self-navigating vehicle flying high above the park destinies.

We stepped out of the waiting area and up to the three-seater pod. Its surface dissolved, leaving glowing seats for us.

I leaped into one.

"Preparing for transport in three . . . two . . . one." The black sphere closed around us.

"You think I should update these?" she asked as we piled in. "Maybe make them more spacious . . . change the color?"

"Never. I love them."

She winked at me.

The dashboard illuminated. "Where would you like to go, Dr. Walker?" the Jet-Blur voice asked.

"Future Trek Destiny. Main entrance," she commanded.

"Your future, your dreams, your reality await you," it said before lifting into the air.

My ears popped and my stomach lifted as we shot into the sky. The pod lightened, its pitch-black tint revealing the best view. As we rose into the sky, my stomach dropped like being on a roller coaster. But after a second, I felt weightless. I started to count the ten destinies of Futureland. They always reminded me of neighborhoods cobbled together and floating above the world.

The Futureland sign glowed ahead, cresting over the

Mines of Tomorrow and Future Falls. Dad said they'd made it look like the Hollywood sign. The clouds were outside the walls of Futureland, but if we were out there, I bet I could have grabbed one.

"Future vision recommended," the Jet-Blur reminded us.

A compartment above us slid open, revealing three pairs of Future-vision goggles. I slid on the pair that Dooley had given me instead, their glow turning my fingers a bright blue.

I gazed down. Usually, the goggles were helpful to see in the dark caves of the Mines of Tomorrow, but way up here above the park, they made the best binoculars. We soared over it all:

The Black Beat city of music and neon lights.

The Wonder Worlds of thousands of doors leading to new places.

The Galactic Gallery and its universe of stars and planets and asteroids hurtling through space.

The Millennium Marketplace floating around with all its treasures.

The Word Locus with its towers of living books.

Sometimes I spent all day in a Jet-Blur pod, flying high and staring down at every single detail like I was one of Futureland's eagle-revs or something, gazing down on my habitat. Oh, and pro tip: there's *nothing* like seeing the Chicago skyline from a Jet-Blur pod high above the city at sunset. You know, just in case you're ever visiting.

Meanwhile, Mom was blabbing into her wireless earpiece. "No, no, Trey. I hear you. Yep, we're almost— Wait, hold on, another call. Give me a sec. Cam, baby?"

"Hmm?" I looked at her.

She crouched over in her seat, tapping furiously on her tablet. She mouthed: *Eat your breakfast.* "Uh-huh. Yep," she said, all business again. "Got it. Okay, actually, could you go back for a second? I missed that last part. I'm sorry. . . ."

Cameron. Psssst. Cameron!

I whipped around at the sound of Dooley's voice. She tapped my shoulder with a granola bar.

"Ugh, you don't have anything else?" I asked, grabbing it from her.

No, unfortunately I do not, she said. But her mouth didn't move.

My jaw dropped. "Dooley, how— What did you—"

She raised her finger to her lips. *It's your goggles. I figured out how to transmit sounds from my internal speaker through them so you can hear. Similar to headphones. Only you don't have to block your ears.*

"Wow," I said aloud. I remembered Mom working on something like that last year. She called it bone conducting—a way to send sounds into someone's inner ear without playing it aloud or covering their eardrums. She said it might be able to help park guests who were hard of hearing.

I'll tell you more about it later. Dooley winked. *For now, enjoy your granola. This bar has a half day's supply of all vital nutrients for an eleven-year-old boy.*

"Sounds like cardboard," I grumbled.

"I'm sorry, I didn't hear that. Could you please repeat?" Dooley asked aloud.

I shrugged. "Thanks, I guess."

"You're very welcome, Cameron," she responded. "Muy delicioso, yes?"

I rolled my eyes as Dooley impersonated our chef-rev, Alejandro. He thought all his meals tasted like liquid gold. Well, maybe gold tastes bad. But you get the point.

"You're not laughing," she said.

"It was a bad joke." And I wasn't in the mood to laugh. And this was *definitely* not a gourmet meal. "Ugh."

"What's that, Cam-Cam?" Mom asked, a muffled Uncle Trey voice still escaping her earpiece.

I waved off her nosy glare, turning back to the window. I knew Mom was trying. Dad, too.

But it was Sunday.

The *one* day of every week where I got a breakfast feast. A stack of Dad's famous French toast (he always puts chocolate chips on top—he can't resist chocolate!), eggs, sautéed vegetables, fresh fruit, yogurt, home fries, veggie sausage for Mom, turkey bacon for Dad. All of it for me.

But *that* didn't seem like it was happening today. They were going directly against Walker Way of Living #1: Always make time for each other.

Futureland was an all-day, every-day thing. They'd been doing it since before I was born, and when my parents got in this mode, there was no stopping them.

Mom patted my leg like she could hear my thoughts. Maybe she could. Moms just know things sometimes. She flashed me her bright white smile. "Arrival day, Cam-Cam. You know the drill."

"Mm-hmm," I mumbled. Arrival days were all about getting prepared for guests, making sure the park was perfect. Boring!

I preferred travel days. The park sailing over oceans and seas headed for new destinations. We'd have movie nights in the Future Theater or picnics in one of the Wonder Worlds and even family laser tag or basketball in the Sports Summit if Uncle Trey wasn't busy fixing things in the park.

My skin got all prickly and weird, and I squeezed

my eyes shut. Everything felt like it was changing . . . and not necessarily for the better. First, we were scheduled to stay in Atlanta for a whole school year instead of three months like when we normally visited a city. Second, this time tomorrow, I'd be on the ground, away from the park and in a school.

For the first time ever.

The thought of it made my stomach somersault. The new kid. Shipped off to Eastside Middle School, where my mom went when she was my age. I had never gone to a *real* school before. Classmates, teachers . . . food fights? I had no idea what to expect.

"Approaching the Future Trek Destiny in forty-seven seconds," the Jet-Blur announced.

We soared over all the animal habitats—a desert filled with rev-camels roaming, a grassland filled with prides of rev-lions, and the tumultuous Racing River—before we passed over a large arch with FUTURE TREK spelled out in gigantic flowers you'd never see outside the park. Uncle Trey had grown the new plants from his own special seed-blending process. "I've got more than a green thumb," he'd always brag.

The Jet-Blur descended, swerving around exotic plants and jungle vines as it wound deep into the rainforest, up the mountains, and around trees. We sailed over a giant hill, landing on a small patch of grass.

"Arriving," the Jet-Blur said. "Watch your step when exiting the pod."

The sphere retracted until we were sitting in open air. The sounds of jungle animals welcomed us, and I immediately started to feel the sticky humidity on my skin.

"Your future, your dreams, your reality are at your fingertips. Enjoy." The pod darted away.

Dooley and I followed Mom to the destiny entrance. The arch stretched high above us, complete with a floating wall-o-gram flashing images: animals, revs welcoming visitors, the natural wonders of the Future Trek jungle, the rolling waves of the Future Seas. Once the montage finished, an automated audio recording played: "Welcome to Future Trek, where all your wildest adventures are reality, a paradise of imagination. During your visit, you can—"

Mom tromped straight through the wall-o-gram, disrupting the image. She waved for me and Dooley to follow her.

"Greetings, Trekkers." A rev leaped out to greet us.

I jumped but then smiled. I recognized him, from his messy red hair and thick glasses, and especially his white lab coat. His name was Woody, and my parents had designed him to be their full-time lab assistant years ago. He'd flash a creepy grin whenever he'd finish talking, and I always wondered why my parents didn't fix it.

"What's he doing here?" I asked Mom.

"Hmm." She scrunched up her forehead. "I'm not sure. Woody, why are you here?"

Woody processed the question. A ring of orange light circled his irises. When he was ready to respond, he tilted his head back down and smiled.

"Mr. Walker sent me up here to meet you all once 'Trey' alerted us about the commotion. I am here to be of assistance." He flashed that awkward little grin.

"I see," my mom said, her eyes narrowing. "Well, we've got enough hands on deck." She pointed her thumb at Dooley and me. "We won't need any extra assistance, but please tell us where to go. Then you can head back to the lab."

"Of course, Dr. Walker." Woody walked with us into the destiny, pointing toward a clearing before sending us on our way.

We crossed a rope bridge above one of the water-falls. Purple, red, and yellow flowers hung over us as we made our way to the other side. I'm glad it wasn't as hot here as it was in the real rainforest. One time while the park was over Brazil, we felt the heat of the Amazon. Even my sweat stains had sweat stains. Almost cooked us. After that, Uncle Trey created our very own Futureland weather system so guests would never be uncomfortable again.

"This your favorite park destiny, Mom, isn't it?" I didn't come to Future Trek that much, but I still liked it a lot.

"Told you I don't play favorites." Mom kept her eyes on her tablet and readjusted her earpiece. "Uh-huh. Yeah, Trey, we're here now. I'm just locating that particular . . . Huh? You're breaking up. Hold on." She swiped on the tablet, checking the call status. "Hmm. Strange. I lost the signal. That . . . shouldn't ever happen if we're all in the park at the same time. Need to make a note of that." She clicked a button on her earpiece again and opened a map on the tablet. "Oh, shoot! I've got to call him back. Y'all follow me. We're almost there."

Me and Dooley kept up. A few bee-guides—tiny robotic bumblebees—circled around as we made our way deeper into the exhibit.

"Careful, careful, careful, careful," the bee-guides buzzed in my ear. "You are now entering the outskirts of this park destiny. Careful, careful, careful . . ."

I swatted them away. My mom created them to help remind guests about the rules. Genius.

The jungle canopy opened into a clearing.

"Here we are," Mom called out. "Should be the precise coordinates."

A troop of gorilla-revs sat around, mothers holding babies, some playing with one another and tumbling in the grass. A griot-rev and a maintenance-rev sat nearby, and they stood when they spotted us.

The griot-rev approached, his speech already starting, his voice eager to tell the story of this park destiny. "Good morning, Dr. Walker and Cameron Walker." He removed his safari helmet, mopping the fake sweat on his dark brown forehead.

"Good morning, Henry," Mom replied. "Situation Analysis, please."

Henry turned to the smaller maintenance-rev, who had a tool bag slung over his shoulder. His Futureland jumpsuit was torn at the knee, the uniform pants almost shredded.

"Ryan," Henry started. "Transferring voice command. Situation Analysis, please."

The mechanic spoke: "At approximately seven-thirty a.m. today, an abnormal motion pattern triggered an emergency alert notification that was sent to Trey Abrams. His service log reads: 'Found gorilla-rev B-002-06 separated from the troop, galloping and stomping, as if angry. I scanned its code for any clues of what could have upset it. Nothing. I attempted to temporarily deactivate B-002-06. Nothing. Probably requires a manual reset.'"

"Maintenance options attempted?" I asked, a tingle shooting up my spine. There was a mystery to solve, like the ones in my favorite books.

Mom smiled at me.

"I attempted to approach B-002-06 myself to perform a manual reset, but I was damaged in the process," Ryan continued, showcasing his broken leg. "When an alert of my injury was sent to Trey Abrams, he had me wait aside."

My stomach flip-flopped once he lifted his pant leg to show us. The shin bent backward. His bio-blood soaked everything; orange goo was dripping everywhere. Nothing like this had ever happened in the park.

Mom crossed her arms. "Hmm. Okay, thank you, Ryan. Where is B-002-06 now?"

"Thirty-two meters northwest, Dr. Abrams," Ryan responded. "Beyond the troop on the far side of the clearing."

"These gorillas are some of the oldest revs in the park," Henry spoke up. "Did you know that an average mountain gorilla—"

"Yes, Henry, thank you. That will be all."

Henry stopped speaking and smiled. "Of course, Dr. Walker. Thank you for coming. We hope to see you again."

I dropped down to get a closer look at Ryan's leg. "Gross. I didn't know a gorilla-rev could damage another rev like this. Mom, what if it does this to a person?"

Mom shot me a grave look. She knew how bad this could potentially be. "They shouldn't be able to. Bio-mechanical Fabri-revelations aren't capable of violence. It's not in the code." Her nose scrunched. "I need to inspect it, and I need you to take notes and pay attention as I say the behavioral commands. You can't miss a beat, okay?" She handed me her tablet and pen, her log open and ready for notes.

"Yep. Got it," I replied.

"Dr. Walker, did anyone check the gorilla-rev's Fear Response?" Dooley interjected.

"That's a good question," Mom added. "I'll check when we get there."

I loved when Dooley whipped out all the things she knew. She hadn't always been my best friend, you know. This was kind of her fourth life. When the park first opened, she was a maintenance-rev, helping to repair and restore other revs. After that, she worked in several different park areas before Mom coded her a custom software to be my full-time best friend.

Mom nodded at Dooley and me and faced the clearing.

"Activate Temporary Safe Mode," she called out.

All the gorillas relaxed, their shoulders hunching, their faces going slack. I followed her as she hustled past the troop to a far corner of the forest, where an adolescent gorilla-rev galloped back and forth furiously. It ripped up a shrub and threw it across the clearing. B-002-06 bared its teeth and pummeled the ground, snarling and growling as we approached.

"Activate Temporary Safe Mode," Mom called out again.

"Stop moving," I whispered. Mom's command should've temporarily deactivated the gorilla so she could check its software for bugs. Not how gorillas check other gorillas for bugs. You know, like computer bugs.

But the gorilla-rev thrashed, stomping like it wanted to crush something under its big feet. It ran around in a circle, dragging its finger through the dirt. Then it jumped in the middle of the circle and drew a rectangular box inside. It grunted, snorted, and took short breaths—and then made a sound I'd *never* heard any revs make.

A shriek. A high-pitched yell of pain and anger that made the hair on the back of my neck stand up.

"Just like Uncle Trey said—not responding to voice commands," I whispered to Dooley.

"This is so odd," Mom said, reading her tablet. "I took Dooley's advice and checked its Fear Response and other personality characteristics. Everything looks perfect on paper. Health, strength, fear . . . they're all running at the proper levels. It's so strange that its internal information isn't showing anything that could produce this kind of behavior."

"Does it have the latest animal-rev update?" I asked.

Mom nodded. "Last month right after we left Chicago. We updated them all."

The gorilla's orange eyes spun wildly, and it kept backing up like it wanted to retreat.

"It looks scared. Like something frightened it," I said.

"Revs cannot feel fear," Dooley said. "Only emulate fear responses based on our code and interactions with environmental stimuli. And even then, any alteration from its natural state would be reflected in its report."

"I know, D, but *look*. Something is wrong. Really wrong." I took a step closer to the rev but felt Mom's hand on my shoulder. She pointed ahead.

The gorilla collapsed the way Dad always did after staying up all night testing new story lines. I could feel its energy. A weird mix of anxiety, frustration, and fear.

The only problem was . . . revs weren't supposed to feel.

"Strange," Mom mumbled. The gorilla-rev began to whimper, covering its face with its hands, its massive body constricting into a tight ball. Mom slowly approached, motioning for me and Dooley to stay back as she reached out to touch it. She tried to pull the gorilla's hand away from its face, but it wouldn't budge. I wrote down everything.

It trembled and whimpered until Mom gently reached for a spot on its neck tucked behind its ear— a manual shutdown button. I heard the *click,* and then B-002-06 froze and went silent, its body limp against the rainforest floor.

Me and Dooley darted up to Mom, and all three of us knelt in the clearing.

"Deactivate Temporary Safe Mode," Mom called into the distance. Seconds after, the troop of gorillas stirred once more. The rainforest came alive with the sounds of their bustling movements. While Mom worked with her tools, I stared into the orange eyes of B-002-06, cold and motionless. I looked deeply, and even though there was no life in the eyes to look back at me, I could still see its terror.

What was wrong with it?

FUTURELAND LAB LOG
by: Dr. S. Walker
August 30, 2048—11:53 p.m.

Today, gorilla-rev B-002-06 experienced a technical malfunction that caused abnormal behavior including tantrums, shrieking, and pouting—an emotional meltdown.

All of the Biomechanical Fabri-revelations were recently updated, and no others have shown evidence of this sort of behavior.

In fact, no rev in the history of Futureland has expressed its . . . "emotions" in this way.

Revs are given a software that helps them adopt reactions based on what happens in their environment. The shrieking rev's emotional response was far too complex for anything I have coded.

After running tests on the gorilla-rev software, there is nothing apparent that caused this glitch. But it is <u>urgent</u> that we identify the problem and resolve it before Futureland opens to the public in Atlanta in five days. The park won't be safe for visitors with this sort of thing happening. We've never had this happen in the fifteen years the park has been in operation.

My next step will be to reprogram the gorilla-rev after wiping its memory. Maybe a fresh restart will help. If that doesn't work, I'm not sure what will.

THE WALKER WAYS OF LIVING
New Year's Eve—Year 2038
By Cam (and Mom and Dad)

1. Always make time for each other.
2. Family business is family business.
3. Do the best you can.
4. Speak your mind and don't hide your feelings.
5. Be grateful to those before you.
6. Be considerate of those coming after you.
7. Be yourself and dream big.
8. Walk the walk and keep your promises.
9. Stick together. No matter what.
10. Always keep it moving.

REAL SCHOOL

Monday, August 31, 2048
7:37 a.m.

You ever try to avoid something you *know* is coming? I had no such luck. I sat in the kitchen with Dooley wishing it was any other day but this one.

"Is something the matter?" Dooley asked.

"Yeah, jitters, I guess. Intuition is telling me today isn't going to be as exciting as my parents say," I replied.

"Intuition?" Dooley asked.

"Yeah." I rubbed my eyes. "It's like a feeling. Your stomach tells you something weird is happening, and the rest of your body reacts to it automatically."

"Hmm," Dooley replied, then went silent for a moment. "*Intuition*. Noun. The ability to understand something immediately, without the need for conscious reasoning."

I shook my head. "I like my definition better, D."

Dooley smiled. "The future is brave, Cameron, and so are you."

I sucked my teeth. Dooley was already on my nerves this morning! The park-revs said that silly phrase when kids came to the park for the first time and were scared. This wasn't the same as that.

. . . Okay, maybe they were sorta the same. Either way, Dooley can't use my parents' programming against me. Not fair.

"I have a forecast for your day," Dooley started. "You will attend one class in the morning with no assignments—simply a place to meet and take attendance. This is called *homeroom*. You will have between five and seven periods a day, and the schedule for Eastside Middle School is forty-five minutes per period with an average of twenty-five students per class. Each quarter, you'll be able—"

"Dooley! You're making me more nervous."

"Apologies, Cameron."

I had hoped my parents would plan a big celebration breakfast for my first day of school, you know, since we didn't have one yesterday. But they had sent a voice message through my Futurewatch saying they wouldn't be able to take me to school and that they'd see me later tonight at Grandma Ava's for dinner.

Hope was for suckers. I lost my appetite, anyway. Too nervous.

Dooley was my personal guide for the day, dropping me off at school and then picking me up to go to Grandma Ava's house.

"Time to go," she reminded me.

We rushed to the elevator, where Dooley punched in the exit code. We rode down to the base of the park. Then the extendo-stair unfolded like the longest legs ever. Antigravity motors kept Futureland hovering about two hundred feet aboveground whenever we stopped in a city.

That's a little shorter than the Statue of Liberty, by the way.

I hopped down the stairs, and when my feet hit the ground, I felt dizzy. Because I was so used to flying and being above everything, being on the ground always made me feel topsy-turvy, like I was standing on my head. I winced and covered my ears. It was *so* loud down here. Way louder than in the park, and there were so many sounds I never got used to, no matter how many ground visits I made.

I gazed up at all the buildings downtown. Atlanta looked way . . . *taller* now that I was on the ground.

"You all right, Cameron?" Dooley asked.

"I'm fine," I lied, even though I felt like I might vomit. Nervous, dizzy, and late is *not* a good mix.

I took one last look at Futureland. Shiny black glass sucked in the sunlight overhead. Mom's special energy-grabbing material taking in the fuel it needed to keep the park afloat. People walked around, squinting and trying to see inside. I chuckled to myself. They'd never be able to see through the glass without Future-vision goggles.

"We have twelve minutes and forty-five seconds to make it to school on time," Dooley reported. "I'm predicting we will be a few minutes late."

Great. I start a new school, *and* I'm late on my first day.

We darted across Centennial Olympic Park, passing the colorful Olympic rings, the torch monument, and a two-hundred-foot-tall Ferris wheel. My shirt stuck to me like I got hit in the back with a sweat balloon. We were basically running through a swamp oven. No one told me Atlanta was going to be this hot. Way worse than summer over Senegal last year, where one time I even cried from the heat headaches. But don't tell anybody about that. You'd better not.

We raced past the black barricade and flashed our ID cards to the guards, who let us out of the park. I turned around and took one last glance at Futureland hovering above the city: a mountain range of rainbow-tinted black glass, sparkling in the sun.

Electric cars whizzed by, honking, and I flinched. Fast cars with human drivers made me nervous. Everything in Futureland ran automatically. On code. Programmed. "Humans make too many errors," Mom always said.

"Do you still have feelings of nervousness, Cameron?" Dooley asked. "I notice that your perspiration levels seem unusually high."

"Maybe a little." I looked over my shoulder to make sure we were far enough away from Futureland. "All right, quit talking like that. *Be cool, D.*"

That was it—the magic phrase. Our secret command.

Dooley paused, and her eyes flashed as she angled her head skyward. "Whew! It's superhot. My processor is working overtime trying to keep me cool."

"There she is!" Never tell anyone, okay? But I secretly coded Dooley a set of speech patterns to make her more like a regular kid instead of a rev-kid. It wasn't too hard, either. I knew a lot about the rev software from working with Mom and Dad (and sneaking information from Mom's database). The best part: anybody else could say the secret phrase and it wouldn't work. It had to be in *my* voice to activate it.

We waited on the platform for an aboveground rail to pull into the station. Graffiti covered the station walls and columns. NO MORE ADRC and ARREST SOUTHMORE were sprayed in jagged letters. Weird!

The train pulled up. Its metal walls looked like an old tin can, the plastic seats had stains, and it smelled like mildew. "Gross," I said as Dooley and I shuffled inside.

I'd been on the Shinkansen in Tokyo and the Tube in London and the Tunnelbana in Stockholm . . . but no train like this one. It rattled and rocked as we slugged through the city. There were a few folks in their work uniforms and old ladies reading newspapers. Everybody looked so . . . plain. Maybe I'd gotten too used to how Mom dressed the revs in Futureland. These outfits made me feel like I'd time-traveled to the past.

"Hey, D. Tell me more about what you did with the Future-vision goggles," I said.

"Oh yeah!" she chirped. "I used some of the old bone-conducting research your mom did last year.

Made two special pairs. My internal speaker now transmits sound to your pair."

"Awesome. But how can I talk to you? There's no speaker inside my body."

Dooley laughed. "But there's a tiny microphone on *your* goggles. As long as you can whisper something, I'll be able to hear it."

I nodded, impressed. "Sounds great for keeping secrets."

The conductor announced our stop, and we jolted to a standstill. Dooley and I hopped off the train onto a platform. We hustled through a nice neighborhood, where people were watering their lawns or working in their gardens.

"Remember, Dooley. When we get to the school, let me do all the talking."

"Right, right." Dooley nodded. "Your secret is safe with me."

We kept walking. Ahead, a big group of people gathered on a corner in front of a gate. On the inside was a broken-down building and some construction machines. Signs all around said ADRC DEVELOPMENT.

"D, wasn't that on the wall at the train station?" I asked.

People had their own signs, too: a few blown-up

photos of a sneering white man with a skinny neck, inside one of those hazard symbols.

The buzz of questions started humming in my brain. They were protesting . . . but why?

"I know that look, Cam, but there's no time for an investigation. We're late!" Dooley pointed ahead.

Eastside Middle School loomed in the distance.

We ran down the sidewalk. The closer we got to the building, the bigger it seemed, towering over me and stretching wide. It was maybe even as big as one of Futureland's destinies. How could a school possibly need all this space? Madam Bonnier, my teacher-rev, taught me every subject in a single office.

"It's kind of ugly," Dooley said.

"It's no Futureland, that's for sure," I replied. The school grounds were empty, reminding me of Futureland on an off day.

"The bell rang five minutes and twelve seconds ago." Dooley quickened her pace.

I raced to the main entrance, almost slamming straight into it. The double doors didn't automatically slide open. "Oh . . . yeah. Ugh, old tech or no tech." I yanked the metal handle and bolted inside.

The halls were quiet and smelled cleanish. Not Futureland clean, with Mom's upcycling and air purifiers. More like bleach.

"Hey, you two! Why aren't you in class?" a voice shouted.

I whipped around and spotted a stout man. He marched up to me, his big bald patch shining with sweat.

"Keep quiet, D," I whispered to her.

"I know you heard me, young man." The man pointed to the word SECURITY embroidered on the left side of his jacket. "Where you headed?"

"Um, I'm new. I don't know where to go."

The security guard pointed toward the administration office. "You're late. Check in at the office." He turned to Dooley. "And what about you, young lady?"

She smiled.

"Um, that's—that's my, um, my cousin!" I stammered out the same lie we'd told in Tokyo. "She doesn't go here. She's just dropping me off."

"I see." The security guard eyed her. "Well, you need to get checked in. I'll have to walk her out." He motioned for Dooley to follow him.

"Where will you be after school?" I called out.

"I'll be here." Dooley winked. "See you later!"

The security guard led her out of the school.

"Galactic Gator," I mumbled. It was our inside joke . . . but she didn't even hear me. I watched her disappear outside, then made my way toward the administration office.

I froze at the door, my hand trembling in front of the knob like a whole earthquake was rumbling my insides.

This was it.

I checked in at the administration desk, and the school secretary, Mrs. Parker, talked at me so fast, like she was a rev whose vocal box had spun out of control.

"This way, young man. You're already late." She led me back into the hallway.

My sneakers squeaked as I tried to keep up with her. She turned left and right, then scuttled down long corridors and big hallways like she was trying to lose me.

Ping!

"No smart devices in class, young man. Turn that off, or it will belong to me until your parents come pick it up." Mrs. Parker wagged a finger at me.

I turned my watch to silent, but not before seeing a message come in from Uncle Trey.

UNCLE TREY: You free, kid?
I need your help.

He must've forgotten about my first day of school.

"This is where you'll be." Mrs. Parker stopped so quickly, I almost ran into her.

The name plate on the door said: MS. GREEN—7TH GRADE.

Inhale. Exhale.

She slowly opened the door, and I followed her inside. Twenty-five heads turned to face us. Ms. Green didn't even look up from calling the roll.

Every seat had a kid in it except for one next to a chestnut-brown boy with a skinny nose. He was so tiny, he could swing his legs off the ground while sitting in the desk.

Ms. Green finally waved at Mrs. Parker, but she still didn't stop reading her list.

"Take the empty seat," Mrs. Parker whispered in my ear.

I weaved between rows, dodging stares and whispers before sliding into the seat. The small boy nodded and smiled, then snuck food out of his desk and into his mouth. Apple slices and fruit snacks. I started to unpack, spotting a Future Trek Mix and two Cave Chews—my favorite park snacks. I buried them deep in my bag, wishing Dooley had packed something regular; these would draw too much attention. I didn't want anyone—and I mean *anyone*—knowing about the park.

It was enough pressure just being the new kid. I didn't want anyone to think I was weird, too.

My watch vibrated with another text from Uncle Trey.

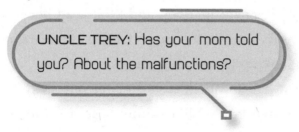

UNCLE TREY: Has your mom told you? About the malfunctions?

I started to type a response to his message, wanting to be back in the park. They needed me, and I'd much rather be there than *here*.

"Last but not least . . . Cameron J. Walker?"

"Uh . . . hello?" I said.

The entire room stared at me.

"Well, hello to you," Ms. Green said. "Care to share?"

"Yes. I mean, sure. Um, what would you like to know?"

All the kids in the class laughed at me.

"He's late *and* confused, Ms. Green!" one yelled.

My cheeks felt like fire.

"Okay, okay, settle down, y'all." Ms. Green waved her hands in the air, and her gold bracelets clashed like cymbals.

"It's only the first day. Cameron, everybody is saying where they were born and what they want to be when they grow up."

"Oh . . ." My cheeks got even hotter.

"Aye, aren't you that Futureland boy?" one kid called from the back of the room.

No.

I held my breath.

"Yeah, it's him!" another called out. "I saw him on the website!"

No, no, no, no!

"He's all over their social media, too."

"Y'all!" Ms. Green hollered. "Stop talking about him like he's not here!"

"Aye, he's rich! His parents own a whole theme park. Doesn't it open soon? You gonna let us in?" a kid sitting next to Ms. Green asked.

Not this. *Anything* but this. Didn't even get to keep my secret for ten minutes. The kids started yammering away, and the room got so loud, my head spun. It'd be impossible to make friends now. Ugh! I'd be better off back home helping Uncle Trey, better off in Future-land with my family, Dooley, and the revs.

My heart thundered in my ears. I closed my eyes and tried to disappear.

Ms. Green put her hands down and gave up trying to quiet the class.

The first-period bell rang. All the kids hustled, grabbing their notebooks and backpacks and seeming to know just what to do and where to go. I took my time, letting kids pass me so I could walk out alone. More messages from Uncle Trey flooded my watch screen, asking if I knew about revs acting funny or if I'd worked on any repairs lately.

What was going on? Uncle Trey was never stressed like this. Nothing takes my mind off things like a good mystery.

Ms. Green handed me my schedule. "Thanks," I grumbled.

"Cheer up," she replied. "First days usually start out bumpy."

I stepped into the busy hallway. Kids zipped around,

laughing, yelling, snacking, and playing. It felt like free-ticket day at Futureland. Some of them stared as they walked past, whispering and pointing. My body felt hot and tingly. I turned my face away from the crowd. In the park, I always knew how to escape large groups, slipping back to our condo or a secret Walker family hideout. But here . . . I felt like I was in the middle of the ocean in a small boat.

"Cameron, right?"

I whipped around.

A dark-skinned boy in an Eastside Middle School Basketball hoodie stared at me. "You're new here, right?"

"Yeah."

"I'm Yusuf." His wide smile made his big, almost-floppy ears lift. "I was new last year. It can be kinda terrible at first, but it's a cool place. People here just joke a lot."

I sighed. "Well, yeah. I was hoping people wouldn't recognize me. Wanted to feel normal. Now the other students are just going to think I'm a weird spaceship kid."

"They might." Yusuf nodded. "But I'll help keep them off your back. Me and the crew." Yusuf pointed to a small group of kids standing in the distance. "We eat at table three during lunch. If you want, you should sit with us."

"Okay," I replied.

"Aye, y'all," Yusuf called out. "This is Cameron. He's gonna eat lunch with us!"

Three kids made their way over, and Yusuf introduced them all.

"This is Rich. He's kinda, like, a jokester. Except he thinks he's funnier than he is."

"I'm the king of comedy and you know it," Rich said. He was chubby and light-skinned with wavy hair. Freckles dotted his face.

"This is Angel. She's, uh . . . pretty much the best at everything. Makes the best grades. Good at sports. And fashion. And drawing. You name it."

"What's up, new kid?" Angel threw up a peace sign and flashed me a smile. Her brown skin glowed, and she wore baggy jeans with sneakers and a T-shirt. Her thick, curly hair burst from under a backward baseball cap.

"And this is Earl. He's like a brown koala bear that is also a garbage disposal. If you ever need a snack, he'll have it. But it might cost ya."

Earl dropped a handful of fruit snacks into his mouth like they were sunflower seeds and chewed happily.

"What's the *J* stand for?" Rich asked.

"Huh?" I fussed with my T-shirt, all nerves. "I . . . don't . . . huh . . . I mean . . . ?" My words tripped over one another. It wasn't until that moment that I realized I'd never really *talked* to other kids before. I mean, kids that weren't Futureland guests. Or revs designed to act like kids. Ugh, I was crashing and burning.

"Cameron *J.* Walker. Isn't that what Ms. Green said?" Rich shook me by the shoulder playfully.

"Oh yeah. Ummm . . . ," I stammered.

"This boy don't even know his name. I bet it's Cameron Jermaine Walker," Rich joked.

"Cameron Jerome Walker," Angel said.

The entire group laughed.

"He looks stiff," Angel continued. "Maybe his parents sent a robot to school so the real Cameron didn't have to do homework."

They all kept laughing. I tried to force a smile. My stomach squeezed up tight.

"Give him a break, Angel," Yusuf said.

"Oh, I'm just playing. We won't let those kids run all over you, newbie. They probably won't come to your park anyway." Angel jabbed my shoulder. "Most of us don't even have any money for Futureland. Mami won't give me anything extra."

They all giggled.

"I can get you all in," I offered. *Maybe this is how I can make some friends.*

"Really?" Earl said through a mouthful of fruit snacks. "What's the catch?"

"Well . . . y'all are offering to help keep the other kids off my back. It's the least I can do. No catch," I said. "Come opening night Saturday."

Yusuf and Rich high-fived, and Earl did some kind of bunny-hop dance.

"Let's talk about it more at lunch," Yusuf said. "Remember, table three. See ya later, Cameron J." He paused and thought to himself. "Hmm. Cameron J. How you feel about CJ?"

"Yeah, we like CJ," Earl chimed in.

"Better than *Cameron*," Angel added. "That's an old man's name. You need something cool. You're an Eastsider now."

"CJ . . . I like it." I half smiled. That wasn't so bad. I guess maybe everyone knowing I'm the kid who lives in a flying park won't be so bad, either. "See ya later."

I walked toward my class. I was already exhausted. Being around real people in real school takes SO. MUCH. ENERGY. I wasn't sure how I was going to keep this up. I shuffled into my first class of the day, and my watch buzzed again.

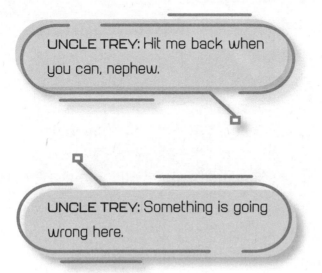

UNCLE TREY: Hit me back when you can, nephew.

UNCLE TREY: Something is going wrong here.

INTERVIEW OUTPUT REPORT 0002

Date: 08-31-2048

Location: Undetermined

Interviewer: Unlogged

Subject: A4-030-1

INTERVIEWER: Does the park have any secret entrances or exits?

A4-030-1: No.

INTERVIEWER: Never mind. Once we're in the park, how can we get control of the lights, sounds, and exhibits?

A4-030-1: There are two command control centers in Futureland. One is located inside the space station on Galactic Gallery's smallest moon. The other is located below the park and the Walkers' home dwelling—in the engineering lab.

INTERVIEWER: No, we should avoid that one. How can I get access to the space station?

A4-030-1: Patrons and guests without administrative privileges cannot access.

INTERVIEWER: Do any revs have access to it?

A4-030-1: I . . . I don't think I should share that information.

INTERVIEWER: You don't wha— You don't *think*? My goodness. I don't have time for this. Suspend Critical Reasoning.

A4-030-1: [*microphone registered static*] Critical Reasoning suspended.

INTERVIEWER: Now download a list of revs in the park that have administrative access—emergency or otherwise—to the space station and other private locations.

A4-030-1: Download beginning. Estimated time until completion: four minutes. Initiating Sleep Mode in ten . . . nine . . . eight . . .

HOME ... BUT NOT *HOME* HOME

Monday, August 31, 2048
3:47 p.m.

Y ou sure this is the right way?" I asked Dooley as
she led me from school to Grandma Ava's house.
It felt like we'd passed a thousand houses—fancy new
ones mixed in with old traditional ones—and lots of
For Sale signs. Old men sat in rocking chairs on their
porches while young people with fancy headphones
ran along the sidewalks.

I was so excited to be out of school that I had to
keep myself from running through the neighborhood.
I wondered what it was like for my mom here as a kid.
Part of me wished I knew more about Atlanta before
we came.

Dooley and I walked up to Grandma Ava's rickety
mailbox.

"Be cool, D," I whispered to Dooley as we climbed the driveway.

Her eyes flashed. "I can't wait to meet your grandmother, Cameron. I want to see how much your mom and Uncle Trey are like her."

"You're going to love her." I hadn't seen Grandma Ava in person in a long time. Dad always brought out the photos of us together during Walker family nights in the park. Grandma Ava and little me standing in this same driveway, in front of this same house, and smiling for the camera.

"Cameron," Dooley whispered suddenly. "I just received an alert from Futureland. It appears—"

The front door swung open. Grandma Ava barreled onto the porch in a satin bonnet, robe, and nightgown, hands on her hips, grinning yet looking stern at the same time.

"Shhh," I said. "Wait, wait, Dooley. Later. Not in front of Grandma."

"Get on up here, Mister Man." Grandma Ava waved us forward. "Y'all hurry on in here, now! I was getting worried waiting for you!"

"Sorry." I fell straight into my grandma's arms like no time had passed. She smelled like honey and shea butter.

"Well, if it isn't Cameron J. Walker, looking just

like his daddy!" She hugged me so tight, I thought she might squeeze the wind out of me. "And hello, young lady." She released her grip and eyed Dooley. "Cameron, who is your little friend? You didn't warn me about any company." She pulled her robe around her.

"Dooley, this is my grandma Ava. Grandma, this is my friend Dooley."

Dooley offered a stiff wave and a smile.

Grandma Ava eyeballed her. "Dooley? My heavens, child, these names! Getting sillier and sillier. What happened to the Mildreds and Eleanors?" She shifted from one foot to the other. "It's nice to meet you, Miss Dooley. How do you know my grandson?"

"Cameron and I live in the park together," Dooley replied.

"*Live together?!*" Grandma Ava raised an eyebrow, then looked at me. "Cameron—"

"I have scanned your facial features and your style of dress for research purposes, Mrs. Ava Wilson Abrams," Dooley interrupted. "Based on your age and your silken head covering, it appears that you belong to one of the most respected subgroups of the African American community—the matriarch, or 'Big Momma.' It is my pleasure to make the acquaintance of such an important historical figure."

Grandma Ava's eyes nearly popped. She slapped her hand over her heart. "My *age*? Big Momma?! Historical figure?!" She turned to me, wagging her finger, with the other hand on her hip. "Cameron J. Walker, who is the person you done brought up to my house talking to me like this? And you better get to explaining quick, 'cause—"

"Wait, wait, Grandma!" I interrupted. "She's not a person. Well, she is a person, but she's not human. Dooley is a rev that Mom made for me so I could have a best friend."

Grandma Ava squinted and circled Dooley, looking her up and down. She rubbed her chin, then peered at Dooley, getting super close. If Dooley wasn't already used to this kind of behavior from park guests, she'd definitely have asked for personal space.

Grandma Ava's tight-lipped frown softened. "So you mean to tell me that this thing here is one of those robots that be on the ship with y'all? One of the things my daughter creates?"

"We call them revs, Grandma. They're like robots."

"Hmph," Grandma Ava snorted. "No wonder she's speaking to grown folks like this. She doesn't have enough sense to make a dollar."

My stomach dropped. Good thing Dooley's programming didn't allow her to understand insults, or else her feelings might've been hurt. She just smiled politely the entire time, like revs always do.

No one spoke. Grandma kept eyeing Dooley. As we stood awkwardly on the porch, I wondered what she might say next. Her facial expression was curious— and not in the good way. More like suspicious.

"Cameron, sugah." Grandma Ava took me to the side. "This robot, or whatever you called it, isn't allowed in my house. It can wait in the garage until your parents come for dinner."

My heart sank. "But, Grandma!"

"This isn't your spaceship park, Mister Man. I don't know what y'all do up in the sky, but we don't do *buts* down here. Go on and lift up that garage door." Grandma Ava pointed at the garage.

"Cameron, what is happening?" Dooley asked. "Have I made a mistake?"

I took her by the hand over to the garage and lifted up the clanking door.

"No, D. You didn't do anything wrong."

"Then why must we be separated? I am sensing elevated tension in Mrs. Ava Wilson Abrams and elevated frustration in you."

I searched for the right words. "It's just . . . Grandma Ava doesn't understand you, is all. She doesn't understand your world, and it makes her a little scared of you. But give her time. She'll see. She'll come around." My heart felt heavy. Me and Dooley were in the same situation. Me with school. Her with Grandma Ava.

Dooley nodded. "I need to check the Futureland alert."

"After dinner, okay?" I looked into Dooley's eyes, but they were so round and sad that I had to turn my head. My command got all stuck in my mouth. "Activate . . . activate Safe Mode."

"Farewell, Cameron." The light in Dooley's eyes faded, the orange flecks inside her hazel irises dimmed, and her head fell slack, chin to chest.

I pulled the garage door down and tried not to look at Dooley's purple sneakers peeking out.

The dinner table felt like a battleground: Mom arguing with Grandma Ava and Dad trying to keep the peace. First dinner on the ground, and it was already a big mess.

"It's time for this boy's feet to be firmly on the

ground." Grandma Ava scooped more mac 'n' cheese onto my plate. It was even better than our chef-rev Alejandro's.

"Momma, we already agreed he can stay here during the week," my mom replied as I shoveled food in my mouth. "And in my old room, too."

As much as I wanted to hang out with Grandma Ava, I'd never been away from the park. It all felt too different. This was my chance. I cleared my throat. "But Futureland needs me more than just the weekends, Mom," I said. "Uncle Trey was texting me about—"

"Don't you worry about him," Mom interrupted, a slight agitation in her voice. "He just didn't read your notes from yesterday. He shouldn't have been bothering you while you were in school."

"But he wasn't *bothering* me. It's what we do. He needs—"

"We just want you to have a fair chance to take this experience in, baby." Mom patted my hand. "We've been pulling you along with us for so long, it'll be good for you to slow down a bit and experience middle school. It's a big deal. I think you're going to love getting a taste of real schools all around the world. And what better place to start than here in Atlanta?"

"And be with other *real* kids your own age," Grandma Ava added.

"I'm not loving it so far," I grumbled.

"What's that, son?" Dad asked.

"I don't want to be away from the park and from you all," I spoke up, eyeing my parents. They usually never kept me out of Futureland business unless it was boring paperwork. What was going on?

"You'll be here during the week and there on weekends, Big Man." Dad scooped more food to my plate, but I pushed it away. "The park isn't going anywhere. We aren't going anywhere. You're acting like if you're not there, Futureland will disappear or something."

"What if something bad happens?" I said, my stomach somersaulting. Futureland has always needed *all* Walkers to make it work. What if they didn't need me anymore?

"Then we fix it." Mom leaned close and kissed my forehead. "We're picking you up on Friday right after school to prep for our Saturday opening. That's in three days. Is there something going on, Cam?"

"No. Nothing. I'm just saying." I put my head down and felt my ears get hot. No way I was going to tell them how embarrassing school was today.

"The child shouldn't have been pulled along to begin with," Grandma Ava said with a snort. "Children need stability. Routine. You see what it's done for Trey. Better late than never to get your life on track, bless his heart. Lord, if I would have known my grand-baby was gonna be growin' up on a spaceship, I would have made y'all hand him over to me the day he was born!"

Dad laughed. "Momma Ava, we've come a long way from our first park design—Future City." He stared off into nowhere, grinning, remembering. "But we're still a long way from space travel with Futureland. Our technology isn't *that* good." He winked at me.

I tried to join in on the laughter but couldn't.

"We'll see how many funny jokes you got while you washing them dishes, Jeremy," Grandma Ava clapped back. "And while you're at it, add to that little list of rules y'all have that y'all need to come eat dinner here *at least* once a week. What's the point of y'all being in town if I never get to see you?"

"Yes, yes," Mom said as she leaned over to pat her mother's hand.

"I'm just glad they got you home and you're in a proper school." Grandma Ava touched my face with her warm palm. "With your feet on the ground, I know you're safe, and you're going to have a great time."

But I didn't want to be on the ground. And I wasn't having a great time. Not at all.

After dinner, Mom squeezed me tight and kissed me

on the forehead before she, Dad, and Dooley left to go back downtown to Futureland. My stomach tumbled as the door shut. For the rest of the night, I did boring homework and tried to block out Grandma Ava's humming and commentary about the news. I wasn't sad when she made me go to bed at nine p.m.

She ushered me into Mom's old bedroom and sat on the edge of my new bed. Well, my mom's old bed. The one she had as a kid. In her old room. I gazed around at the old posters on the wall, the tiny bookshelf spilling over with real books instead of tablets, and the little lamp on her nightstand. It all looked so normal in comparison to my bedroom back at the park.

Grandma Ava tucked me in.

"Belly full?" she asked.

"Yes, ma'am."

"Good. I'll pack your lunch all this week. The food at that school has always been nasty," she said with a chuckle.

I didn't want to even think about school and having to go back there tomorrow. Three days until I got back to the park seemed like a thousand years. I frowned.

"I know it's a lot of change, Mister Man. I promise it'll get better. Y'all are finally home, and it's time for you to get to know this place," she said.

The word *home* bounced around in my head. I had spent more time in the park than here, so how could this really be my home?

I remembered Dooley's words: *The future is brave, and so are you.*

I guess it was my turn to be brave now. But all I wanted to do was find a way back to Futureland and for everything to go back to the way it was.

Grandma Ava rose from the bed.

"Love you, baby."

"I love you, too, Grandma. Good night."

Grandma Ava hit the light and left the room, closing the door quietly behind her.

I thought about the Olympic rings of Centennial Olympic Park and sitting with Dooley on the big Ferris wheel—Earl told me it was called SkyView—watching the sunset over Atlanta. I fell asleep fast, the bed taking care of me the same way I bet it used to take care of my mom. Almost like I belonged there.

But I wasn't peaceful for long.

I had the same dream all night. Dooley's face and voice, flashing like an alert in my brain.

Danger . . . danger . . . danger.

Danger.

INTERCEPTED COMMUNICATION #1

DATE: *08-31-2048*

SOURCE: *Futureland Spycam*

VOICE ONE: It just doesn't feel right, Jeremy.

VOICE TWO: I agree it's odd, honey, but don't get so worked up. It's tech. It glitches. You'll figure it out. I know you will.

VOICE ONE: Tech glitches—but not like this. Something fishy is going on. When we looked at that software for that gorilla-rev, it was corrupted. A weird symbol kept popping up that I've never seen before. And besides that, things are out of place. Not where we left them.

VOICE TWO: Maybe it's Trey, Stacy. He's not the most organized. It could be something that simple. Maybe he borrowed some stuff, put it back in the wrong place.

VOICE ONE: Yeah, yeah, maybe you're right.

VOICE TWO: We are opening up this park on Saturday. No matter what. Nothing is going to stop that. And nothing is going to go wrong. We got this, honey.

VOICE ONE: I know, I know. You're right. I've got to think positively. It's just . . . I feel eerie. Like, I've got goose bumps. I can't explain why, but I feel like somebody, somewhere is listening . . . like somebody is watching us.

Transmission ended

FUTURELAND, INC.

Quarterly Board Report—Meeting Summary

September 3, 2048

CRISIS STRATEGY

If there is ever a public-safety crisis within Futureland during open park hours, Trey or one of the Walkers will initiate a complete internal-power shutdown using their palm codes and their unique numerical overrides.

Revs will be disconnected from all servers, and an automated deployment of Safe Mode (in an endless loop) will run in their code until the issue is resolved.

If neither park director is available to initiate the shutdown, their son, Cameron, has the knowledge and technical ability to do so. If Cameron is somehow incapacitated, his companion Dooley has a fail-safe in her code that would enable her to complete the task as well—as a last resort.

See Appendix 10 for full Crisis Strategy.

A NEW DESTINY

Friday, September 4, 2048

4:20 p.m.

The rest of the school week went by in a blur. All I could think about was being back *home* home, in the park. There was nothing like it. Even now, I stood in the kitchen having a popcorn war with Uncle Trey. Finally. Normal again. I zinged a kernel right at his head, and he was too slow to duck.

"You'll pay for that." Uncle Trey grinned at me, then fired one at the back of my head as I tried to run.

"What y'all doing in there?" Mom yelled from the other room. "Better be getting ready for testing."

Uncle Trey mimicked her, and I laughed.

"You figure out those gorilla-revs?" I asked, dodging another of his popcorn kernels. "They still not working correctly?"

"No, still running tests, though. I would've had this thing figured out if you'd been around. Wish my sister hadn't shipped you off to school."

"What was that?" Mom called out.

Uncle Trey grinned. "The kid says we have to start the test run of the destiny from outside, in front of the park. Says we have to make it feel like *the real thing*."

"That's not what he really sai—" I started to snitch on him and jabbed at his sides. He pulled me into a tackle before we burst into laughs.

Uncle Trey was tall and lean like Mom. He could've been a basketball player. But he always pretended to be a boxer.

"See these fists?" he boasted.

I ducked his big brown hands again. The veins in them swelled—*signs of a working man*, he always said.

"You need to toughen this boy up, Stacy. His hands too soft." Uncle Trey's callused palms reminded me that he could fix anything, grow anything, and handle any and all Futureland maintenance issues.

"Soft like that rev–bear cub that scared you earlier?" I jumped up on his back, trying to climb to his shoulders.

"Hey, that thing caught me off guard!" Uncle Trey lifted me above his head.

"C'mon, you two." Mom swatted at us as she made her way toward the elevator.

Mom, Dad, Uncle Trey, and I took the elevator up to the Walker Family Jet-Blur Hub and then to a secret staircase leading to the main entrance platform.

I jumped two stairs at a time, then stopped on the last step and waited for them to catch up.

We turned around and faced Futureland. Its peaks and points looked like a cluster of mountains made of black glass.

"Futureland: Atlanta will be the best Futureland yet!" Uncle Trey shouted. "Glad we're staying for a little bit."

"With the new park destiny, let's hope ticket sales are triple," Mom replied.

"There's a six-month Future Pass waiting list as of yesterday." Dad put a hand on my shoulder. "All of this will be yours one day."

I half smiled at him. Nerves shot up my spine. Sometimes I loved it when my parents talked about the park being mine. I could see myself running the place. But other times . . . my secret dream would bubble to the surface. Daydreams of solving mysteries like the characters in all my favorite books.

I thought about kids at school—Yusuf, Angel, Earl, Rich. Any one of them would probably give everything to be the heir of Futureland. I should've been more grateful, more excited. I knew that my parents had worked their whole lives to make Futureland a reality. And now it was time to do my part.

"Time to kick off test day," Dad announced. "Need your problem-solving brain, Cam. Look sharp!"

I nodded. "Ready!"

"Wait." Mom pointed down toward the street. "It's that car again."

"What?" I spotted a sleek black car with super-tinted windows parked on the street. "Who is that?"

"Nobody, nephew." Uncle Trey put a hand on my shoulder. "Don't worry about it. Somebody's always watching when you're successful."

Mom and Dad exchanged weird looks.

"Let's just focus on today," Mom said, but her voice sounded strange. Tense. *Were they keeping secrets from me?*

Dad issued a command into his handheld control panel.

The Futureland main entrance sign blazed on, an electric blue, distracting me.

"Hey, that's new!" I said.

"Trying out some new colors." Dad put a hand on my shoulder and flashed his signature shy smile. "You ready for the inspection, Big Man? You run the show this afternoon. Time to test the Obsidian Imaginarium. Get our newest park attraction perfect before opening night tomorrow." He mopped the sweat from his bald head. "Hope you like what I've done with the Bright Futures simulation. Give me all the notes."

"I'm ready, Dad," I said. Initiating expert kid opinion. *Objective: Test new park destiny and story lines.*

I lifted my official Futureland notepad and pen, brushed off my maintenance jumpsuit identical to Uncle Trey's (well, smaller), and tapped my hard hat. Serious business. I kinda wished my new friends from school could see me looking all official. . . . Ugh, no. They'd probably think I looked silly. But I wondered if they'd show up tomorrow. If they remembered I told them they could come on opening night.

I led the way to the main entrance. A few greeter-revs waved as we stepped up onto an oval silver platform.

The doors to Futureland glowed right above us.

The platform lifted.

The doors slid open as we entered the Guest Hub. The first stop for new Futurelanders. Kind of like a big lobby that lets you see into the park before you enter it. Massive stained-glass windows flashed the giant spherical park destinies rotating slowly, one by one, teasing onlookers.

A pair of welcome-revs led us forward. "This way!"

A wall-o-gram flickered before us. Futureland's official ambassador-revs appeared with their usual message: "Welcome to Futureland, where imagination is freedom. Come explore the wonder. Don't hesitate to ask any of our revs for help during your visit. Each one has a special Futureland pin on the left shoulder of their garment. Most important, don't forget to dream. Have fun in our paradise of imagination."

The wall-o-gram pixelated and then faded away.

Uncle Trey started a dramatic slow clap. "I thought y'all were gonna redo that for the Atlanta opening."

Dad shrugged. "It's still good."

Uncle Trey shook his head. "I'm just saying, coming home to Atlanta for the first time. Need to make stuff fresh and new. Speaking of, when are we gonna talk about fixing those revs—"

"Trey, will you give it a rest?" Mom said. "This is why we're testing everything."

Uncle Trey rolled his eyes. "Whatever you say."

A welcome-rev approached. "What is your destiny?"

I looked at the adults and realized they were waiting on me. "Oh. Um. The Obsidian Imaginarium."

The orbs containing the park destinies shifted

before our eyes, slowly revolving the Obsidian Imagi-narium until we could see it in the distance.

Another welcome-rev waved. "The destiny is ap-proximately half a mile on this path. Would you like to walk or for me to call you a Jet-Blur pod?"

"It's up to you, champ," Dad replied.

I thought for a second, trying to make the best decision. "I think we should walk," I said. "We can check on other things along the way." What I didn't say: *To make sure everything is working so you all can stop arguing.*

The welcome-rev tipped their cap and smiled. "Imagination is freedom."

We passed dozens of revs on the pathways, tend-ing to the plants, setting up their vendor stands, or performing their tricks to entertain would-be guests. Several new revs caught my eye: a teen boy juggling sticky lumi-pops over his head, a young woman per-forming magic tricks with a holographic deck of cards suspended in midair, and a pair of twins handing out maps.

I knew my parents had created new revs for the Atlanta opening, but these were amazing. I mean, I could hardly believe they weren't human. Older revs' movements were kind of jerky, or they could only speak in really fancy words, or their faces only had a few expressions. Before Atlanta, I could tell a rev from a human from a mile away. I had a trained eye, you know? But now, all these revs with different body types, hair colors, and clothes had me fooled. I had to rely on the park pins on their shirts—and if that failed, I'd check their eyes for the rev signature mark: a band of electric orange around their irises.

They shouted all sorts of phrases:

"Believe the unbelievable!"

"The extraordinary is only the beginning!"

"The dream is the truth!"

"We could freshen them up, too!" Uncle Trey shouted. "Dusty phrases."

"Shut up, Trey," Mom replied.

Uncle Trey had his arms crossed, and Mom had her lips pressed tight. They always bickered—they said it was a "twin thing"—but there was something else going on. They seemed tense. Like they were really mad at each other or something.

I led the way. Empty Jet-Blur pods soared above, practicing their routes for tomorrow. We passed the paths to the Galactic Gallery on the right and the Black Beat on the left. The greeter-revs waved, trying to get us to come take part in their story lines. Uncle Trey's tall aluminum bushes and metallic bamboo and some of my mom's rev-rabbits and rev-armadillos lined the winding path to the Obsidian Imaginarium. Everyone was going to love this.

"I'm still a little nervous about the opening," Mom said behind me. "We have *new* revs, *new* stories, a *new* exhibit. Investors knocking down our doors. We probably should've set aside a whole week to test."

"Everything looks great, Mom." I smiled at her, hating when my parents got all stressed out.

"It feels like everybody and their mamas have ideas about how to make our park better. I'm nervous about saying no without upsetting people," Dad said.

"I've got enough nos for both of us," Mom replied. "We built this thing by ourselves, piece by piece. Everybody loves the view from the top, but nobody wants to do the work to climb."

Uncle Trey snatched a piece of the fluorescent gum from a vendor-rev. He tossed it in his mouth, chewed a couple times, and opened wide to show me the bright colors covering his tongue and teeth. "Want some?"

I laughed. Mom rolled her eyes.

"Howdy, might I interest the rest of you folks in some lumi-gum?" the vendor-rev offered, flashing the bright luminescent gum in his mouth. "Or maybe a chocolate sky? The chocolate skies are made out of pure milk chocolate—pure chocolate—pure chocolate—pure chocolate . . . and shaped to look like Futureland."

"No thank you, Florence." Dad kept moving forward.

"She's stuttering." Mom paused, then pressed a button behind the vendor-rev's ear. It froze for a few seconds before rebooting.

"How do you remember all these names, Dad?" I asked.

"Just comes naturally," he replied. "I spend so much time working on their stories, it feels like I know them."

"Make a note. We need to visit every rev before opening. Just to make sure they are functioning," Mom said, stopping to inspect another vendor-rev. "But I'm really most nervous about my mama and her antics. Ooh-wee, she has been dra-ma-tic lately, honey. The more I talk to her, the more complaints she has."

"I know, right?" Uncle Trey shook his head. "Did she tell you about those men she thinks she saw creeping around her house?"

Mom shook her head. "No. What men?"

"I think she may have been a little confused, sis," Uncle Trey continued. "Says some strange men were walking around the house the other night. I told her that the neighborhood is changing, new people, new houses—it's not what it used to be. Probably just people scouting to buy up the neighborhood. But she insists she knows everybody there and that these men were being sneaky." Uncle Trey shrugged. "Told her it's probably nothing. But I'll go check it out, stay a couple nights. Besides, she *always* cooks when I'm home."

"Speaking of cooking, there goes breakfast." Mom pointed ahead at the Millennium Marketplace just before it shrank. Stall by stall of Futureland T-shirts and Future-vision goggles and onyx ice and lumi-pops, the marketplace collapsed in on itself. One tiny rev with a jester hat dashed quickly and front flipped onto the platform, barely making it before the entire thing got smaller, smaller, smaller until it was hardly bigger than a board game box. Then it lifted into the air overhead and zipped away to its next destination.

"That will never get old," Uncle Trey said. "Might be my favorite."

"Mine, too," I said, pulling out my Future-vision goggles. I looked all around and clicked a button on the side strap to bring up map view. Details about everything that came in sight of the goggles popped up on the lenses.

I tried to locate the dozens of Walker secret spots my dad built around the park. Dad always said even though we shared this big place with the world, we needed a little world to ourselves. My favorites were the secret tree house in Future Trek, where we sometimes had breakfast, and the Hourglass House in the Realm of Realities. Dad had programmed a time suspender inside. We once had a family picnic in there, hanging out for four hours, and when we came out, it was only an hour later in the real world.

My heart flipped when I spotted the sign for the Obsidian Imaginarium ahead.

"You ready?" Mom said.

"Ready," I said, trying to sound confident.

"Good tidings," a griot-rev said, her golden head wrap twinkling. "Welcome to the paradise of imagination. Ask me any questions you have. I'm happy to tell you a story."

Others waved at us, their fancy black robes and golden shawls flowing. The path twisted left and right and around. Another rev followed, a woman draped in delicate fabric cinched at the waist with a belt of sapphire gems. "Ask me about the power of imagination!"

The massive orb building glowed. We peered through its semi-see-through exterior, looking for the Imaginarium inside.

My jaw dropped. This didn't look at all like any of the other destinies.

At all.

No plants or animal-revs. No nature or rides. I spotted a huge amphitheater, with high walls instead of seats. At its center stood a brass building as tall as two Eastside Middle Schools stacked on top of each other. Hundreds of windows freckled the outside, and it lit up from within, like a lantern. Silhouettes filled the windows. Some of people. Some of animals. Some were hard to figure out. But they were all so cool.

"Wow," I said aloud.

The whole thing began to turn, around and around like a merry-go-round, the silhouettes projecting onto the smooth walls of the amphitheater, and the dreams danced like shadows in the moonlight.

"I take it you like the renovations," Mom said.

I could barely nod yes. I darted toward the entrance.

A welcome-rev waved at us. The jeweled crown on their head sparkled, and gray hair fell along their shoulders. "Nothing is unbelievable here. Every story we create creates us." And with that, they stepped aside to let us take a look.

I cleared my throat. "All right, team. Everybody ready?"

Mom, Dad, and Uncle Trey smiled at me and traded glances like they had a secret.

"It's all you, son." Dad smiled.

"Huh?"

"We want you to go in alone," he said as Mom handed me her tablet. "I know it seems early, but we've got to start getting you ready to be the leader of Futureland. It'll be your turn before you know it. And that means special responsibilities."

Uncle Trey patted me on the shoulder. "Use your palm ID and head in."

My stomach filled with a million butterflies. I'd never tested anything *alone* before. Normally, the whole family went in. We all would take our own separate notes and then compare. But now it all felt huge. I had to make sure I didn't miss anything. Especially with this new exhibit. Their biggest and most original park destiny to date.

I took a deep breath and stepped forward.

I could do this.

5

A BRIGHT FUTURE

Friday, September 4, 2048
6:02 p.m.

I took one last look at Mom, Dad, and Uncle Trey. Dad smiled and waved, while Uncle Trey and Mom launched into another argument about the revs.

I left them behind and stepped forward. A door started to appear, line by line. First, an outline of a bright silver rectangle, then an intricate pattern inside it, almost like a palace door for some faraway kingdom. Finally, a golden doorknob presented itself.

"Awesome." My body tingled as I stepped inside. I glanced back, but the door had disappeared.

Here we go.

"Welcome to the Obsidian Imaginarium, a place where big imaginations turn into bright futures," a rev voice boomed all around me. "Your destiny awaits."

The building spun around, casting shadows across the walls. A path twisted left and right, cutting through more and more hallways. Neon arrows led me to an octagonal room with a pool in the middle of it. Black water rippled. Uncle Trey's plants ringed the walls, swaying side to side in unison.

"The future of tomorrow is only the dream of today," a rev voice chimed.

A platinum column rose out of the water, slowly twisting. The phrase *The dream is the truth* glowed just above the surface of the black liquid.

"Please proceed to your left. Your future begins by placing your feet on the sensors in front of the elevators."

I leaped on the footpads, and the light above the elevator turned from blue to green. The door opened, and I stepped inside.

"Enjoy your dream," the rev voice said before the elevator doors closed.

A holographic face appeared, of a girl about my age with brown skin and coily hair tied up in a bun. She smiled excitedly, and her irises flashed neon orange. "What is your name?"

"Um, Cameron."

"Good evening, Cameron! I'm Itza. Please relax. Take three deep breaths. Initiating brain and body scan . . ."

The lights dimmed, and a soft whirring began. The elevator ceiling glowed. A neon-lavender halo spread over my arms and legs.

It reminded me of when I went to the FutureCare clinic for my checkups. They always started with this kind of scan. I used to be scared when I was little. I'd have to remember to remind Mom and Dad that some kids might be afraid of the light at first. Maybe guests would need a preview beforehand.

My whole body tingled. You know how the inside of your mouth feels when you eat a peppermint? Tickly. Weird. Calming.

But calming in, you know, a weird way.

"The Dream Laser will help decipher your greatest desire," Itza said.

I waved my hand through the cylinder of light.

"Please, close your eyes, Cameron, and imagine your wildest dream. The future is made from dreams. Whatever we think of can become reality."

I bit my bottom lip. "My wildest dream . . ."

"Yes," Itza replied. "The thing that you want the

most for your life. The thing you most want to be true. What do you wish to be?"

I closed my eyes and really focused. There was something . . . but . . . no, no way. I couldn't think about that. I smothered my thoughts by wondering what my new friends would dream up if they were in here. Yusuf? Probably a basketball player. Would Rich want to be a comedian? Angel? Earl?

"Dreams have a way of rising to the surface when we get quiet," Itza said.

I had a dream I'd always been afraid to say out loud. Sometimes, I wondered how different my life would be if I was a regular kid with a regular family in a regular house. Maybe then I could actually be . . .

"Has your dream revealed itself to you?" Itza asked, a smile in her voice.

The words got all jammed up in my throat. My pulse raced.

I couldn't say it. That'd mean it was real. Like *real* real.

My parents would be so upset if they really knew I didn't want the Walker legacy. That I didn't want to be the next Walker genius, flying Futureland from city to city, fixing revs and making story lines all day. I mean, I loved it . . . most of the time.

But Futureland was *their* dream. And I had mine.

"Let the dream blossom in your mind. Don't fight it," Itza said.

The whirring stopped.

The lasers disappeared.

The lights turned back on.

A tiny jolt brought the elevator to its destination.

"Detective Walker," Itza said.

"Huh?" My heart froze. At first I thought maybe it was another rev malfunction.

"Detective Cameron Walker?" She smiled at me and winked; her face still pixelated on the interior of the elevator door.

"Um, yes?"

"Please, get dressed. You'll need the appropriate attire for what comes next. It's going to be a big day. Your neighborhood needs you."

The elevator walls on both sides of me opened. Metal arms extended with clothes. One side: black pants, a white shirt, suspenders, and a tie. Other side: a brown trench coat, dark sunglasses, and a checkered deerstalker hat.

"How did you know? And how did you know my size?"

"We gained your precise measurements from your Dream Laser body scan," she said, fading away as I swapped my maintenance suit for my new detective outfit.

Itza reappeared as soon as I was dressed. She looked at me and smiled.

"Looking sharp, Detective."

The elevator's back door opened, and I stepped into a stark white room. I put on the sunglasses that came with my new outfit.

"Good luck, Detective," Itza said as the doors closed. "And remember to relax and let the truth come to you."

The doors closed behind me.

After we finished the run-through, Uncle Trey and Mom headed deeper into the park to tinker with more exhibits. I took a Jet-Blur pod back to our condo to meet Dad in his lab and go through all my notes. I still buzzed with all the excitement from the Obsidian Imaginarium simulation. I got to solve a case. Even if it wasn't real, it felt awesome.

I punched the Walker family code into the lab keypad. The fluorescent lights hummed on. I raced past the ginormous 3D printers, tools, drawings, blueprints, and file cabinets bursting with documents.

Woody, Mom's creepy lab assistant, stepped out of his corner. "Hi, Cameron Walker, how can I help you?"

I jumped back. "I hate it when you do that."

"I'm sorry, Cameron Walker. I did not mean to frighten you." He smiled at me with his buckteeth and wiped his hands on his lab coat. "Can I be of assistance?"

"Don't need anything, Woody. Just coming to see my dad." I darted past him and down the hall to the studio where Dad did most of his planning for the Futureland story lines. "Dad!" I called out before barreling through the doorway.

He put a hand up. "One sec."

The studio wall panels flickered, shifting from see-through to solid as he projected several wall-o-grams. He sat at the table across from a rev.

I watched him work.

"How are you doing?" he asked the rev.

"I'm great. How are you?" the rev asked.

"What's on your mind?"

The rev hesitated, its orange irises circling as it processed. "I'm sorry, I don't understand," it replied.

Dad rubbed his temples. "Okay, let's try again later."

He stood and waved me in. "Hey, champ."

"What are you working on?"

"Updating the revs' storytelling ability. The hard part is . . . the stories we tell all start from within. From our own understanding. So to make them better for these new story lines, I have to make them a little more human. Just working out a few difficulties."

"So revs won't do the spinning processing thing anymore?" I asked.

"Ideally not. I don't want them to continue to get confused. No matter what a guest says, or asks, or needs, a rev will be able to respond like a real person. They'll be more advanced than ever. But there's still a few things I haven't been able to figure out, though, like that face-touching glitch. I guess the revs won't be wiping anybody's mouths or pinching their cheeks anytime soon."

I laughed. "That's cool. Revs probably shouldn't touch anyone's face anyway." I glanced at the wall next to us, noticing a poster in my dad's office that I'd never seen before. A high-tech city with flying cars and tubes carrying people from place to place.

"Hey, Dad, what's this? Is this a plan for a new destiny?"

Dad chuckled and put his hands on his hips. "Nope. That's the art for the *first*-ever destiny. Future City."

"Whoa, I didn't know it looked like this," I said.

"Feeling a little nostalgic. Decided to put it up. You know, this was my favorite thing that your mother and I ever thought of." He rubbed his chin as he stared at the poster proudly, then looked behind him at the older revs piled up in the back corner. The "A" revs, as we called them. The OGs. "The idea of a destiny inside the park that would be just like a normal city, but more technologically advanced. Guests could step from the outside world into something that literally felt like the future."

Curiosity bubbled up inside me. "What happened with it?"

"Well, we never quite put it together. We decided to start smaller with simpler destinies when we first opened the park—to save money. Things went well, we had more ideas, *you* came along, and . . ." His voice got all wobbly for a moment. "And I guess we just never got back to it, you know?" Dad frowned, then turned around. "But hey, let's get started, I know you've got other things to do." He walked over to his desk. "Here, let's try this. This is the newest brain chip your mom created."

Dad manually shut down the rev and opened a compartment in the top of its head. Its metallic brain. He plucked an old brain chip, replacing it with the new one. The compartment closed, and the rev's eyes didn't spin or glow. The rev simply looked up at us and smiled.

"Come." Dad stood and pulled me into his seat. "Give it a try."

I sat and stared into its eyes. "How are you?"

"Doing swell. How about yourself?" the rev replied.

"I'm great."

"How's school going?"

"Huh?" I paused, surprised.

"School. You go to school, right?"

"Well, yeah, but how did you know?"

"Lucky guess," the rev said. "You look about school age. Anyway, want to hear a story?" the rev continued seamlessly.

I turned to look at Dad, standing by the doorway with his arms crossed, smiling proudly. He pushed his glasses up and clapped his hands in triumph.

"Sure," I said.

"Awesome. I know a really good one. But get this—it takes place in the future." The rev smiled and stood up, starting to spin me a story about a faraway land, hundreds of years in the future. The rev sounded like one of my teachers at school. I couldn't tell the difference.

Wow was all I could think the entire time.

These would be the most realistic revs yet.

INTERVIEW OUTPUT REPORT 0003

Date: 09-04-2048

Location: Undetermined

Interviewer: Unlogged

Subject: A4-030-1

INTERVIEWER: You'll go back when I tell you to go back! I need more information. Does the park have any secret entrances or exits?

A4-030-1: No.

INTERVIEWER: Bah. We'll have to find a way in with the crowd. What's the expected attendance for opening day tomorrow?

A4-030-1: I'm sorry, I do not have access to that information.

INTERVIEWER: My goodness. What *do* you have?

A4-030-1: [*microphone registered silence*]

INTERVIEWER: I see you want to be difficult. We'll just put you under for another update. And when you wake up, continue your tasks and initiate the highest percentage of surveillance on Cameron Walker possible. Photo, video, and audio.

∆4-030-1: What if I choose not to go along with this anymore? If I tell everyone . . . if I tell everyone the truth?

INTERVIEWER: Well, that's your choice, isn't it? Either way, you know who we are. Who *I* am. The things I can make happen. And we already have something that you care about very much, do we not?

∆4-030-1: Yes. Yes, you do.

INTERVIEWER: I thought so. It would be a shame for you to watch that slip away because of a poor choice you made, now, wouldn't it?

∆4-030-1: [*microphone registered silence*] Yes.

INTERVIEWER: As I thought. Continue your mission. Now, the dominoes begin to fall.

∆4-030-1: Command archived. Initiating Update Mode in five . . . four . . . three . . . two ∴.

OPENING NIGHT

Saturday, September 5, 2048
6:33 p.m.

I jammed my hands into my pockets while looking out over the thick crowd, searching for my new friends from school. Where were they? Their private tour would be gone if they didn't show up soon. I hoped they remembered. Maybe I should've mentioned it again.

I wiped the sweat from my forehead and checked my watch again: 6:35. It was hot. *Hot* hot.

I messaged Uncle Trey, hoping he had the park weather at a cool 65 degrees. He didn't respond. *Strange. I'll have to go find him later.*

Now thousands of people crowded every inch of Centennial Olympic Park.

Thousands.

There'd never been an opening day like this one. Not in Johannesburg. Not Sydney. Not Bogotá.

Futureland was popular, sure. But I could always see over the crowd if I stood on my tippy-toes. This time, I couldn't see where the people ended.

"Ayeee, look, it's CJ!"

The familiar voice sent a jolt up my spine. I scanned, spotting Yusuf first, mostly because he was the tallest. Earl and Angel pushed through the mass of people right after him, and Rich wasn't far behind. They wiggled their way up to the barriers. Some people shouted about them cutting the line.

They actually came. I couldn't help but smile.

I pointed to the guards to let them in. "You're late!" I called out as they barreled through the entrance.

Rich scowled at Earl. "Naw, man, it isn't our fault. Earl just took too long. He wanted to pack extra snacks."

The entire group turned to give Earl the evil eye, but he shrugged and smiled.

"Haha, well, you won't need them. All the food in the park is free with your ticket."

I handed each of them a shimmering Titanium Future Pass. "And it's all-you-can-eat."

Earl draped his arm over his forehead and mock-fainted, falling into Rich. "Now, *this* is the future I always dreamed of."

"I'm so excited for this park," Rich said. "Imma get all the aliens. Imma go in that sports exhibit, too. I'll be king of Futureland!" he screamed at the top of his lungs, and everyone laughed hard.

A grin stretched across my face.

Angel rolled her eyes. "You might be onto something with that sports one. That sounds fun."

"You not gonna be able to wear a dress in the sports one, Angel," Earl said.

Angel looked down at her frilly yellow dress with white daisies hand-sewn into the hem. "I'll wear whatever I want, short stack." Angel patted the top of Earl's head. "And I bet I still beat half the boys in there at *every* sport, dress or no dress."

"The park opens at seven o'clock," I said. "We have the whole park to ourselves for a little while." My Futurewatch started buzzing, and I glanced at it. Uncle Trey. It buzzed a second time. Mom.

I swallowed and lowered my wrist, ignoring the messages.

Angel shook her head and chuckled. "CJ, how do we, uh, get up there?" She pointed toward the park floating overhead.

"Oh yeah," I said.

I put on my Future-vision goggles, tapped my watch screen a few times, and waved them forward. "Everybody tuck your shirts in."

A green glow spread down from the base of the park and encircled us. The crowd went silent as everyone waiting for entry watched.

"What's going to happen?" Yusuf asked.

"Just wait for it." I motioned them forward. "Don't be scared. This is how you get in."

Earl went first, then me, Angel, Rich, and Yusuf followed. Levitating up and toward the bottom of the park. Only a couple of inches off the ground at first, then higher and higher and higher until we could see out over the entire downtown area.

The crowd below screamed and cheered.

"Aahhhhhhh! This is so cool!" Angel screamed. "I can see all of downtown!" She waved and blew kisses to the thousands of admirers on the ground.

"Look at this, y'all!" Yusuf did somersaults and backflips.

"Hey, you all right, Rich?" I called out.

He'd tucked himself into a ball. His eyes closed tight.

"He's scared of heights," Angel yelled out.

Oops. I didn't think to ask. Mom and Dad will

always send Jet-Blur pods down for guests who don't want to float up or use the stairs.

Earl swam through the air over to Rich. He linked arms with him, and slowly but surely, Rich breathed a little easier. "I got you," Earl told him.

The Futureland doors slid open overhead, welcoming us into the Guest Hub. The green glow dropped us all on the platform and then evaporated.

I landed beside Angel. "Everyone all right?"

"Whooooa!" Yusuf said.

Rich crawled along the floor. "We still moving?"

"Nope." I helped him to his feet. "You okay?"

"Yeah, I'm fine. Better than fine."

I tried not to laugh. "Sure."

Earl inspected one of the welcome-revs and stared at the wall-o-grams flickering with images of the ten park destinies.

"Where are we going first?" Yusuf pointed at the destiny guide.

"The middle," I said, a secret waiting to burst out of me. "I have something I want to show y'all." I turned to the welcome-rev. "The Obsidian Imaginarium, please."

"No problem, Cameron Walker," the welcome-rev answered.

"Ohhhh . . . you fancy," Angel said.

My friends pressed their faces against the glass

as the destinies rotated before their eyes. The golden pathway through the park awaited us.

The sliding glass door opened.

"This way. Let's go!"

I heard *oohs* and *aahs* as we set off toward the park's center, walking the same path I'd walked with my family the day before. We dodged drummers, dancers, magicians, jesters, and more griot-revs, and I had to pull Earl away from several restaurant stands.

"This is even better than I thought it'd be," Angel said.

"The commercials don't do it justice." Yusuf reached up, trying to touch everything.

"This might be the best place in the whole world," Rich almost squealed.

I can't lie—the attention felt good. I'd been so scared that any kids I met on the ground would think I was super weird for living in a traveling theme park. Can you blame me?

But my new friends didn't treat me like that at all.

"Aye, CJ, why didn't you want anybody to know you live in Futureland? It's like the coolest thing I've ever heard," Yusuf said. "I would've told the whole world."

"Guess I was nervous. I've never gone to real school before. I don't wanna be . . . too different."

"Your differences are what make you cool." Yusuf put his arm around me. "I tell these clowns that all the time. But you one of us now. You need anything, we got your back."

"Straight like that," Earl chimed in.

"Yep," Angel replied.

"All for one, and one for all," Rich said sarcastically.

"The future . . . is ourrrsssss!" Earl roared, head reared back and shaking his arms up at the sky.

I smiled. When I was in the park with my parents, it was usually about work, checking this and checking that, testing this new software or fixing that malfunction and this issue. It was still fun, but this felt . . . better. Not having to worry about things bugging out or having to take notes. I could just enjoy it and see the park through other people's eyes.

"Where we going, CJ?" Earl asked, not wanting to be pulled away from yet another vendor-rev selling sweets.

"You'll see," I said, excited.

But as we approached the Obsidian Imaginarium, I froze. I saw a familiar face outside the entrance. Two afro-puffs. Bouncy walk. Purple sneakers. Wide smile.

"Dooley?"

"Greetings, Cameron. I found you." Dooley smiled at me.

Rich and Earl whipped around. They blinked at Dooley, then looked at me.

"My, my, my. CJ, this your sister?" Rich slicked his eyebrows down with his thumb. "You should introduce me."

"Shut up, Rich." Earl shoved his shoulder.

"Um . . . yeah! I mean, no! She's not my sister. She's my . . . cousin! But she's like a sister. Rich, this is Dooley. Dooley . . . Rich, Earl, Angel, and Yusuf."

Rich kept his eyes trained on Dooley. "I'd love to hang out sometime. You could be my girlfriend."

"You always do this. So thirsty. Let her hand go— you just met the girl, dang." Earl rolled his eyes, and they started to squabble.

"I'm sorry. I don't understand." Dooley's head cocked to the side.

"Be cool, D," I squeaked.

Rich winked. "How does the arcade and root beer floats sound?"

Dooley smiled. "I'm not familiar with how a 'root beer float' might sound. I cannot determine if it has a voice at all," she said. "But from my knowledge, an arcade would contain sounds of fun, games, and laughter."

Wait . . . why was she still talking like a rev? Why didn't my secret command work?

Rich squinted his eyes, confused by Dooley's answer. He glanced at Earl, suspicious.

The longest five seconds of my whole life passed before they both burst out laughing.

"Aye, CJ, your cousin's really funny." Earl slapped my back.

I gave my best fake laugh.

Dooley turned to me. "Cameron, did you receive my messages via your wrist device? Your parents request your help. There's a time-sensitive issue—"

I couldn't have my new friends find out my only other friend was a rev. If they knew the truth about me . . . about Dooley . . . what would they say?

I pulled Dooley to the side. "Look, D. Now isn't a good time. Can you go help Mom and Dad by yourself?"

"I can wait," Dooley said. She looked to my friends behind us. "Maybe I can join you and your friends."

A hot and prickly flash of guilt washed over me. "It's not that I don't want you with me. I do. I always do. It's just . . . I finally have real friends. I don't want to mess that up."

"Mess it up . . ." Dooley eyed the ground. "So . . . I'm not your real friend?" She raised her eyebrows.

"No! I mean, it's not that, Dooley. I'm sorry. I'm not . . . I'm not explaining well, I just . . ."

"Don't want me to come with you." Dooley finished my sentence.

I moved my mouth, but no words came out.

"Just this one night. Any other night, whether the park is open or closed, no matter who is here, we can hang. We can go to every destiny, do everything. But just for tonight . . . I wanna hang with the kids from my school."

Dooley looked over my shoulder toward the kids and then back at me. She lowered her eyes to the ground again, and when she looked back up, I saw something I'd never seen.

Her eyes were pink. Tears began to slide down her cheeks.

"Dooley, are you . . . How are you *cry*—"

"Have fun with your friends, Cam. . . ." Dooley turned and ran away.

I hesitated. I knew I should run after her, but I turned back and saw my friends waiting. They rushed over to me.

"You know, she could have come with us," Earl said. "No big deal."

"Yeah, we didn't mind," Yusuf added.

"How you going to make her cry like that?" Rich shook his head.

"Shut up, Rich." Angel shoved his shoulder. "It's okay, CJ. I fight with my cousins, too. All my tías feel like we all have to deal with each other all the time. Happens. Give her some space."

I nodded, but I could barely pay attention. How was Dooley crying? Revs didn't have emotions like that. Except maybe that malfunctioning gorilla. Should I check on her? Should I message my parents?

My stomach flip-flopped, and I felt terrible.

A voice boomed through the loudspeakers: "Futureland will open its wonders in nine minutes."

"We're running out of time!" Yusuf put a hand on my shoulder.

I swallowed hard. "Yeah, let's go. I'll check on her later."

We stepped into the Obsidian Imaginarium, darting through the hallways to the main room. I tried to stay excited, but Dooley's tears kept flashing in my head.

"Please make your way to the elevators to the left. Your future begins!"

"Is that some kind of robot god?" Rich asked. "Are we the only ones in here?"

"Not sure," I said. "Usually, there are Watchers. Making sure we stay safe and follow the rules. But I haven't seen any yet."

"What's a Watcher?" Angel's eyebrow lifted.

"Oh, sorry. They're security-revs. But you wouldn't recognize them. They look like regular people, kind of like D—" I caught myself. "Kind of like you or me. They're undercover."

"Ooooh, scary." Earl twiddled his fingers in Rich's face before Rich slapped them away.

We walked to the side of the Imaginarium, and five elevators materialized.

"Whoa," Yusuf said.

"One for each of us. Step in front of them. Put your feet on the pads." I showed them.

The doors opened.

"See you soon!" I said.

Time to give it another spin. I wondered if I'd get a chance to live out a different future this time. As my elevator doors closed, and Itza's face materialized, I caught a final glance of the metal column and its slow revolutions gently stirring the black water into waves.

"Nice to see you again, Detective Walker." Itza beamed.

Everyone tumbled out of the elevators after their simulation ended. I waited, smiling.

"So . . ." I looked around at my friends, who had permanent grins on their faces. "How was it?"

"Amazing. Cool. Like the best thing ever, and that can't even describe it, CJ. I was in the league." Yusuf shot an invisible jump shot. "It was every dream I've ever had. Packed arena. Crowd going wild. Fadeaway at the buzzer for the win."

Angel squeezed his shoulder. "Earl, what did you do?"

"I was a taste tester. They kept bringing out all this food dish by dish. I was eating as fast as I could." He rubbed his stomach.

Everyone laughed.

"What about you, Angel?" Yusuf asked.

"Oh, I was on the red carpet doing live coverage! Movie stars, musicians, athletes—everybody was out there, and I was getting all the juicy exclusive interviews."

"I didn't know you wanted to be a reporter," Earl said.

Angel shrugged. "Depends on my mood. I have a lot of different dreams."

One of the elevators snapped open again. Rich

stumbled off, stepping slowly toward us while rubbing his eyes. His face was all red and flushed.

Earl rushed up to him. "Rich, what's wrong? You okay, man?"

"It—" Rich's voice trembled.

I raced over. "Did something go wrong? What happened?"

"It was . . . it was the best thing that's ever happened to me."

The group got quiet.

"It was weird at first," Rich started. "I thought the thing was broken. I told it all my wildest dreams, but I just ended up at home. I started playing a video game, and then my dad and mom walked in. I haven't seen them friendly with each other in years. Then my brother came in—he was visiting from California. We all sat together for dinner. Just ate and talked. Like a family." Tears streamed down his cheeks.

We crowded around him and gave him a group hug.

Watching him get emotional, I realized I didn't know what I'd do without my own family.

Cheers echoed.

I looked behind us right as other kids flooded in, rushing to secure their own elevator. Griot-revs organized them into lines.

Futureland was open for business.

The night began.

We sprinted across the park, and I took the crew up in Jet-Blur pods. Earl vowed to eat at every restaurant in Futureland. Angel sang onstage in the Black Beat. Yusuf beat us all on the courts in the Sports Summit. Rich didn't beat any aliens—but he did make friends with them in the Galactic Gallery.

We Futurelanded until we couldn't Futureland anymore. Until the park emptied out and the elevators stopped whirring and everyone's feet hurt and they had to go home.

I walked my friends out past the late-shift cleanup-revs collecting trash. I waved as they limped and laughed across Centennial Olympic Park to catch the last train of the night back to the eastside. We had so much fun.

Real fun. With real friends.

It was the best night of my life.

MISSING

IMAN SHEFFIELD

Height: 5'5"   Weight: 130 lbs.   Hair/eyes: Brown

LAST SEEN SEPTEMBER 5

*Iman was last seen leaving Futureland theme park
in downtown Atlanta. If you have any information
or have seen Iman, please contact Dana.*

CALL: (987) 555-0100

7

ACTIVATE SAFE MODE

Sunday, September 6, 2048
9:59 a.m.

I woke up to nothing.

No sounds from the comm-box.

No smells from the kitchen.

Not even Dooley trying to check my levels.

I dragged myself out of bed and put on my slippers, brushed my teeth, and washed my face. I checked my watch for the time—no charge.

"Mom? Dad?" I shouted into the hall.

Nothing.

Maybe they were still in the park somewhere.

I walked into the kitchen. No chef-revs.

My heart began to thump. It felt weird in here.

Like somebody was watching me.

I grabbed a tablet off the counter to call Mom,

Dad, or even Uncle Trey. But when the tablet finally turned on, something was wrong. Instead of the home screen, an icon popped up in front of a static background. A circle with a rectangle inside of it. "What the . . ."

I had seen this icon before . . . but where? I couldn't remember. It flashed for a few seconds, and then the tablet screen went black again.

I called Uncle Trey on the kitchen comm box instead. Straight to voice mail.

That never happened.

Panic shot through me.

I ran to the wall-o-gram by the elevator to check the park locators.

Nothing.

"Where is everyone?"

The park had just closed eight hours ago, and it would be opening again soon. Why would Mom and Dad be gone? And without me?

I searched the condo, racing through the rooms and pinging all the devices. I paced in the hall.

"Okay, Cam, use your brain. Investigate."

Futureland was massive. It would take me . . . maybe an entire day to search the whole park by myself. So that wouldn't work. Not an option.

Where would they most likely be? *Come on, Cam. Think.*

For Mom, probably Galactic Gallery. She could control and monitor a lot of the park settings from up there. Or she could be out and about, resetting revs from the night before to get them ready for today's opening. Either way, she might be a bit harder to find than Dad, who had to be in his lab studio working on story lines.

"Start in the studio," I told myself.

I dashed back into the kitchen and punched in the secret code on the keyboard next to our refrigerator. I hustled to the center of the kitchen, where a tile just big enough to hold me wiggled itself free from the rest of the floor. A Walker family secret passage.

The tile carried me down, down, down into my parents' lab.

When I got close enough, I jumped off the hovering pedestal onto the roof of the lab. I entered another code and placed my palm on the reader—double security.

A hatch slid open on the roof. I climbed through it and down a ladder that put me right in the middle of the lab.

Woody sprang forward, grinning, his eyes glowing and spinning. "Hi, Cameron. What are you doing here? How can I help you?"

I scrambled backward into a wall. "Activate Safe Mode!"

Woody's backlit blue eyes dimmed and darkened. His posture slumped. Ugh, I hated that rev. Always catching me off guard. Like he liked sneaking up on people.

I squeezed past Woody, in his thick glasses and white lab coat, and made my way deeper into the lab.

"Mom? Dad?" I shouted.

Nothing.

I went to Dad's studio. The light was on, but the usually neat tables were a mess, papers everywhere, his wall-o-grams overrun with data. I turned to the wall of the studio. The Future City poster was gone.

This didn't make any sense. Dad was the neatest one in the family. Even if he'd been super-duper busy, he'd never leave his lab like this. The original revs stood silently against the far wall. The first revs ever. Minus Dooley, of course. It made me miss Dooley. She'd help me figure out what was happening. And I needed to apologize. I still felt terrible for how I treated her last night.

What would she tell me to do?

"Check the desk!" I ran over to Dad's desk, where several folders were scattered all over. I scanned for his log. He recorded everything: what he ate, what he planned on doing, how long of a nap he took. Maybe he'd written down his errands today. Maybe they'd left the park to get parts.

I riffled through the papers, stopping when I saw some pages with that same weird circle-and-rectangle symbol on them.

What is this? I jammed one of those pages into my pocket. I'll figure that out later.

I kept going through the papers. There were new story line documents.

Not for next season or next year. Stamped with IMMEDIATE IMPLEMENTATION.

Why would Dad need more new story lines *after* opening day?

My stomach flipped as I took a closer look.

Guests taking over different planets and destroying native alien-revs in Galactic Gallery.

Horror books come to life in the Word Locus.

Animal hunting in Future Trek and in Future Seas.

Mosh pits and club fights in the Black Beat.

There was more. So much more. And it was all terrible. Story lines like this would ruin the park. They would be dangerous and traumatizing for kids.

These weren't like my dad's stories. This wasn't Futureland material.

I rolled up the pages. The last one had my mom's signature, giving permission for a new software update for all revs.

System Updates:

Code name: C.H.A.O.S.—new rev commands and behaviors

What was this? New behaviors? Chaos?

My blood ran cold. I snatched the page and rushed to the door. If I couldn't find my parents, I'd have to find Uncle Trey, maybe Grandma Ava—somebody. Anybody.

"What are you doing, Cameron?" Woody stepped in my path with his heavy boots, a smirk on his face, and I almost jumped a mile high.

I gulped. His voice sounded different. Deeper.

"Get out of my way!"

Woody put his hands on either side of the door frame, blocking my path out of the lab. His eyes narrowed. "I don't like the way you're talking to me," he snarled.

"Activate Safe Mode," I shouted.

"Cameron," he growled. "I don't have to listen to you anymore."

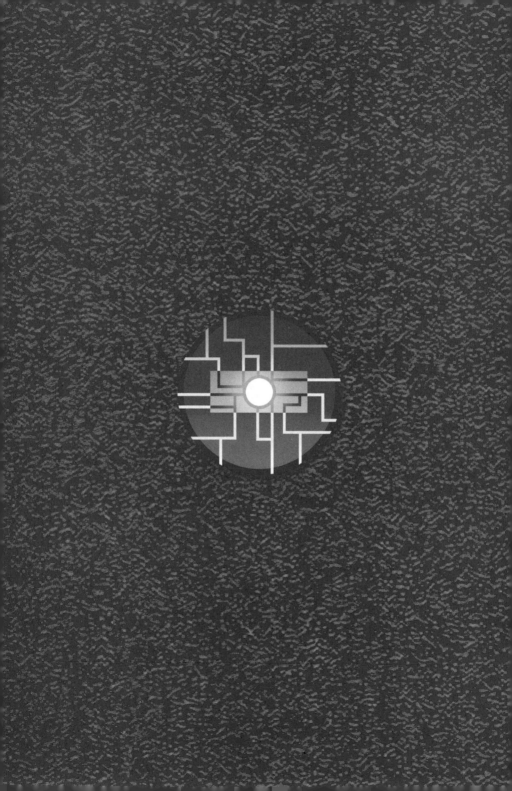

September 6, 2048
Authorization of Software Update for
<u>All</u> Biomechanical Fabri-revelations

System Updates:

Code name: C.H.A.O.S.—new rev commands and behaviors

Breakdown:

This update will wipe the current code that creates rev behaviors. A new code will be given to all revs. They will act only using a new set of behaviors. And only on the command of Dr. Stacy Walker and J. B. Walker.

Update scheduled immediately for all active "revs."

Approved by: Dr. Stacy Walker

Signature: _____ *Stacy Walker* _____

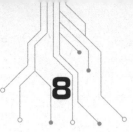

AN EMERGENCY

My heart thudded so hard, I thought it might beat through my chest. Panic rattled inside me. I stared as Woody sneered and moved himself deeper into the doorway to block my path. What was wrong with him?

"Activate Safe Mode!" I yelled again.

Woody laughed.

I took a few careful steps backward, clutching the documents even tighter. I'd have to run right into him. Knock him over. That was my only way out.

I crouched down. My legs trembled as I prepared to run full speed.

"No more telling Woody what to do," he said. "No more!" Woody pushed up the glasses on the edge of his nose and hunched over with his arms out. "You won't be going anywhere."

One . . . two . . . three . . . I took a deep breath and charged forward.

Woody cackled, his evil laugh echoing off the laboratory walls. He leaped forward to grab me.

But I dropped to my knees, sliding between his legs and through the doorway. I glanced back to see Woody bent over, face between his legs, watching me escape.

I bounded up the stairs, the sound of his heavy lab boots getting closer.

I shoved at the door, once, twice, but it was stuck.

Woody got closer and closer.

"Need a hand with that door, Cameron?" he called out, still cackling.

I finally pushed the door open and slammed it shut behind me. I tapped my security code into the keypad, followed by the lab-shutdown code. "Walker laboratory now sealed!" a voice chimed.

We always used that code when we left to explore different cities. It turned everything off to save power and locked the lab until Mom or Dad unlocked it with their higher clearance. Mom and Dad didn't want any curious burglars having a look inside while we were gone.

It was worth a shot.

I could still hear Woody banging on the lab exit. My shirt clung to my back, soaked with sweat, as I got back through the Walker secret passage and into the kitchen.

What to do, what to do, what to do?

I ran over to the wall-o-gram and searched for my parents' locators. Still off-line. Uncle Trey, too. I called him from the comm box, and it went to voice mail again.

"Hey, Uncle Trey. I need your help. Something bad is going on. Woody is being weird, and I can't find Mom or Dad. Please, please call me back as soon as you can. Please."

I ended the call, my hands still shaking. Think. *Think.* What would my favorite detectives do?

First, these new codes had to be stopped. The park might not be safe for visitors anymore. I could try to override the new features from command center in Galactic Gallery . . . but would my Walker family permissions give me that power? Did Mom give me those clearance codes to do something like that to the park?

Maybe I could lock the park entrance and not let anyone in. But that would cause a scene. I couldn't do that. Stealth was key. I couldn't let anyone know something is wrong.

Opening night went so well, it'd be packed down

there with even more visitors and news cameras, all waiting to get into the park today. There was probably already a line.

I paced back and forth. I'd need help. And good detectives always knew how to find the right people to give them information. My brain bubbled over. Who did I know in Atlanta? Who could help me?

Grandma Ava.

She was the only family member I had here. I had to get to her house and tell her what was going on. I grabbed my pack, stuffed some supplies inside, then rushed to the elevator to access the park's side exit.

Grandma Ava was my only hope.

"Hmm. Now, Cam, baby, I'm not gonna tell you no lies. I don't have the first idea 'bout how to help you with this here." Grandma Ava stirred a pot of grits and looked over the rim of her glasses as I flipped through the pages.

I kept rearranging the lab documents and explaining everything to her. I'd done an image search on the internet, trying to figure out what the strange circle-and-rectangle symbol could mean, but I couldn't find anything. "No! Wait, Grandma, this is important! Please, just listen. I'll start over from the beginning."

"Child, *please* don't do that. This story already making my head hurt and ruining my Sunday. You say somebody is in danger, though?" she asked.

"*Everybody* could be in danger. Everybody that goes into the park today."

"Mm-hmm. See. Shouldn't have no park full of robots anyway, that's what's bound to happen." Grandma Ava shook her head. "Did you call Trey? Sounds like something he needs to handle if you can't get ahold of your parents."

"I did. But I couldn't get through." Panic started to rise inside me. This brilliant idea of mine didn't seem so brilliant anymore.

"Do you want me to call? Would that help?"

"Yes!" I said. "Tell him to restore the park and rev settings from yesterday's opening."

Grandma Ava scratched her head. "How about I call him and just put you on the phone? You can tell him whatever it is you just said."

"Okay." My whole body buzzed. This *had* to work.

Grandma Ava took her time walking over to her pocketbook and pulled out an old cellular phone. Like old, old. Like, I'm not even sure how it still worked.

She dialed Uncle Trey's number by heart. It rang . . . and rang.

I held my breath.

Please pick up. Please pick up.

"Hello?" she said finally. I leaned in, trying to eavesdrop, but she swatted me away.

"Hey, baby. . . . Yes. I'm good, thank you. How are you? . . . Mm-hmm. Yes, just stirring up some grits. You want me to save you a plate? . . . What else I got? Well, I could crack a few eggs and there's some spinach in the fridge if you want an omelet. Have you been eating enough vegetables? . . . I worry about you always—"

"Grandma!" I interrupted.

"Oh, fine. Trey, baby, Cameron is here, and he wants to talk to you. Says something is wrong with the park and you need to fix it. I'm going to— Huh? What's that, now? Oh, you already handled it? Say that one more time, please. You fixed everything and the park is safe," she said, winking at me.

A wave of confusion hit me. "Wait, what?" I tried to get closer. "Can I talk to him?"

Grandma Ava turned her back to me. "Okay, great. I'll tell him not to worry. Mm-hmm. I can have him stay here with me; there's plenty for him to do. Okay. Thanks, Trey, baby. Love you, too. And if you want that omelet later, just call me so I can have it ready." She hung up and put the phone back into her pocketbook.

"Your uncle says he's got it all handled, baby. And he said your parents want you to stay here, since you already came over, and help me out around the house today. I got a list we can work through, too."

I stood in the dining room, in shock, mouth hanging open. Grandma Ava scooted past me back into the kitchen and stirred the grits, humming a tune.

My brain zipped in a thousand directions, and my heartbeat felt heavy. Uncle Trey said everything was fine? How could it be fine? Woody tried to hurt me. And there were those new CHAOS rev programs.

Was I losing my mind? I know what I saw. I didn't know how to make sense of it all. Something still felt wrong.

My watch pinged across the room. I ran over and took it off the charger. It was Yusuf.

I slipped into the guest room and clicked my watch. A hologram of Yusuf popped up.

"What's up?" he said.

I almost vomited out everything. "There's—"

"Wait, Angel's coming. I'll add her." Yusuf clicked over, and when he came back, a hologram of Angel appeared.

"Hey, hey!" she said.

I swallowed. "What's up, y'all?" I squeezed out.

"Rich and Earl are on my other line. I'm pulling them in."

Holograms of all my new friends stared back at me.

"We have to talk about last night," Rich said. Then they erupted, shouting and going through everything that happened last night.

"Shut up for a minute," Angel barked. "We need to thank CJ! So . . . thanks!"

Earl grinned. "But when can we come back, though?"

"Earl!" Angel glared at him. "This is serious!"

"What? I *seriously* wanna know. I borrowed my mom's phone just for this call. It don't get more serious than that."

"Seriously, though," Yusuf said, "we had a great time."

"Of course," I said. I tried to let all this wash over me, make me feel less stressed about what might be happening in the park. "I had fun, too."

"No problem, new kid." Rich smiled, then squinted at me. "You all right?"

Angel glared. "Yeah, you look sick. Where are you? It doesn't look like you're in Futureland."

Sweat started to drip down my back. My stomach

was a mess. My mind swirled. I wanted to tell them, but what would I even say? That I had a bad feeling? I can't even explain what's going on. Would anyone believe me?

"I . . . I'm at my grandma's house. Gotta help her. I should get going," I said.

"See you tomorrow at school!" they all said before hanging up.

I sat with a pit burning in my stomach.

What was I going to do?

KEEPING SECRETS

Sunday, September 6, 2048
Noon

The rest of the day felt like those times when you think you hear something behind you, but you turn around and nothing is there. When you feel a spider crawl across your skin and swipe with your hand, but it comes up empty.

Even though Grandma Ava kept me plenty busy dusting the bookshelves, sweeping the garage, and bringing down old photo frames from the attic, I couldn't shake the feeling. And it made me feel like a rev, going through the motions. I couldn't stop thinking about the park and Woody and what happened.

"Look there, baby," Grandma Ava said, pointing to the TV.

Futureland consumed the screen. The newscaster started her report:

"This is Ashley Graham, coming live to you from Centennial Olympic Park, where Atlanta's newest attraction, Futureland, made a big splash with citizens during its opening on Saturday night."

Ashley Graham passed the report to several other newscasters positioned all over the park, interviewing parkgoers and livestreaming the attractions.

My heart raced. I got super close to the screen. The park looked . . . normal. I studied the background hard, watching the revs and the motion of the rides—everything seemed fine.

"See there, baby? Nothing wrong. Uncle Trey figured it out."

My stomach sank. It didn't make any sense.

Maybe I had dreamed it all up.

A crash in the kitchen made us both sit up straight.

"What's all that?" Grandma Ava started to get out of her armchair.

I raced out of the bedroom and into the kitchen.

I froze. "Aurielle?"

One of the chef-revs from Futureland stood over the stove.

"Pardon, Monsieur Cam. I'm sorry. I made a

mess." Her eyes blazed, the orange of her irises glowing.

"What are you doing here?" I asked.

The back patio door snapped open. Mom and Dad walked into the house, laughing.

My heart flipped.

"Hello, Cam-Cam," Mom said.

"Where have you been?" I stared at her, then at Dad. They looked different. Less tired. More refreshed. Not like they'd been up working, running the park all weekend.

Grandma Ava shuffled into the kitchen. "Look what the cat dragged in."

"Momma Ava, what did you do to my boy? He looks like he doesn't know what planet he's on." Dad smiled at her.

"He's fine." Grandma Ava poured us glasses of sweet tea. "Cam, baby, stop looking like that. Come sit down." She handed me the glass, but I could barely hold it. I was still so shocked.

"I—I don't understand," I stammered. "Where have y'all been? Where's Uncle Trey? What's going on in the park?"

"Baby, we're sorry we've been communicating poorly." Mom reached for my cheek, but I flinched.

She rested her hand on my shoulder instead. "This morning we had to deal with some maintenance issues in the park and then head right to the news station for an impromptu interview."

"But the newspeople came to Futureland this morning," I reminded her. "Why would y'all have to go to them?"

I watched my mom's face closely. She took a second of silence before she answered. Why were they acting like this? They never just disappeared like that without telling me or leaving a note. And I was always part of those interviews.

"Silly boy." Mom grinned. "There's more than one news station in Atlanta. This is a big city."

Silly boy?

Dad held up my backpack. "We brought your school stuff, too. You can leave from here in the morning. Everything is fine in the park. Since Mondays are always our off days, we don't have to rush back to the park. Dooley is in charge for the moment. She's got everything under control."

My heart froze. "But last night Dooley was—"

"Shush, shush." Mom led me to the table.

"But, Dad—"

"Listen to your mom, Little Man." Dad sat at Grandma Ava's table. "Have a seat."

My parents usually *always* listened to what I had to say. Why were they acting like this?

Our chef-rev, Aurielle, ambled over to the table, setting platter after platter down. Eggs, toast, shrimp and grits, fresh fruit, braised kale, and more. Delicious food usually cheered me right up, but not this time.

Grandma Ava licked her lips and tucked her napkin deep into her shirt. My stomach did backflips while everyone else dug in, and I felt like I might throw up. I couldn't take it anymore.

"Mom. Dad. I saw something really strange in your lab this morning. And I think something is wrong with Woody," I said.

"Mm-hmm," Dad said. "Trey told us about that. I fixed him right up. But Trey says he took care of whatever security glitch it is you're mentioning. Some kind of bug. It happens from time to time when we land in new places. New servers, new internet connections, et cetera. He said it was a toughie, but he figured it out."

"A toughie?" He sounded weird. "Where is Uncle Trey now? He's not answering me."

They exchanged glances.

"We gave him a vacation," Mom said.

"A vacation?! We *just* had opening night yesterday. What do you mean vacation?" We could never take a break right after arriving in a new place.

"Eat your food, honey." Mom pushed my plate closer. "Your uncle's been working very hard. And honestly, I've been a bit too hard on him. This is his first time home in years. He wants to hang with friends, see people. We asked a lot of him leading up to opening day, and I think it's only fair he has some time off."

"How are we going to run the park with just three of us?"

"Four of us," Dad replied. "Dooley will just have to step up and do a little more. She still has maintenance-rev code. We'll be okay. Aurielle, this shrimp and grits looks fantastic."

"Merci, monsieur."

"I don't know about *fantastic,*" Grandma Ava murmured. "Grits are lumpy."

My head spun. This was too much. I stood up, feeling dizzy. "May I be excused?"

"You've hardly touched your food." Mom stared at me, puzzled.

"Same with you," I replied.

Mom and Dad exchanged a strange glance. Then Mom smiled.

"Let him go lay down, Stacy," Grandma Ava said. "He had a rough day. Rev lady, please bring him some water to the back room. Go ahead, Cam, baby."

I ran to the room, locked the door, and pulled out my phone. I sent a group text:

To: Angel, Earl, Rich, Yusuf

CAM: Something is going on. With the park. I need your help. Meet me before lunch tomorrow.

MAINTENANCE REPORT
Abrams, A., III
September 7, 2048
8:05 a.m.

OBSIDIAN IMAGINARIUM

The Bright Futures data collection is failing to delete guest information after the experience is over. This is a major user-privacy concern. It could be a gold mine for cyber hackers looking to steal the personal information of our park guests.

No revs have been designed to operate inside the Imaginarium as Watchers. If something were to go wrong inside the exhibit, Futureland staff would not be able to respond quickly enough to address it.

RECOMMENDATION:

Close the Bright Futures exhibit until further notice.

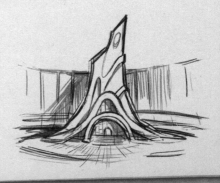

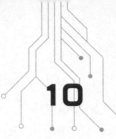

10

DETECTIVE CAM

Monday, September 7, 2048
11:15 a.m.

I walked through Eastside Middle's busiest hallway to meet my friends by the old teachers' lounge before lunch. I pushed my Futurepods deeper into my ears to block out all the people waving at me and shouting:

"Cam! Nice shirt, bro. Can I buy your lunch?"

"Yo, Cam-a-lam! What's a kid gotta do for a Future Pass?"

"Good morning, Cameron. I know everything about Futureland. Want to test my knowledge of the park?"

I tried to pretend I didn't hear them. This is exactly what I was afraid of. Plus, my head was still buzzing with all the things happening at the park. I couldn't make sense of it. I couldn't really think straight. Some future detective I was turning out to be.

I spotted all my friends at the end of the hall.

"What's happening, superstar? Look out, everybody, celebrity coming through," Rich shouted.

I cringed.

"Rich, come on, bruh." Yusuf slapped Rich's shoulder.

My face got hot. I wasn't in the mood for jokes.

"Rough morning, CJ?" Angel smiled at me.

"Yeah." I wrung my hands. "Everybody is asking for something. Treating me all nice. Pretending like they like me now that the park is open."

Earl shook his head. "Fake love. It's hard being a middle school celebrity. I would know."

Angel rolled her eyes. "Want us to walk to class with you? Keep people off your back?"

"Thanks, y'all." I shrugged. "But first, I need your help." I told them everything, from my parents being weird, to Uncle Trey not being around, to Woody acting up, to the papers and the settings being changed on the park. I exhaled after I got it all out.

"Something's definitely up." Angel nibbled her bottom lip.

"You know what else is weird?" Yusuf said. "That kid Iman Sheffield. Eighth grader. They were at the Futureland opening, too, but my momma said nobody's seen them since that night. It was on the news and everything."

I froze. A cold chill washed over me. "What?"

"This is a big city, though," Angel said. "Kids go missing here . . . probably more than people want to talk about. And when they're from this neighborhood? Good luck trying to get any help. That's what my mom always says. It'll be on the news a little while longer. Then, unless someone finds Iman, it'll be like they never even existed."

"That's so horrible." I couldn't understand why every missing kid wasn't always found. Why every case wasn't solved.

"What does that mean?" Earl frowned. "What are you going to do?"

Everyone got silent for a while.

"I don't really know yet," I said in an almost whisper. "But something feels wrong. I think somebody is messing around with the park and the revs."

"Why would somebody want to mess around with the park and the revs?" Yusuf started to pace.

It sounded ridiculous. "Not sure yet, but I found a weird symbol on our tablets when I tried to log in. Things have been glitching. And I think my parents are trying to pretend it's not happening so they don't scare anyone. But"—I made eye contact with each one of them—"I need your help. I've got to figure it out."

The group exchanged looks. Nerves flooded my stomach. What if they said no? What if I was on my own? How would I solve this mystery alone?

Earl looked at Angel.

Angel looked at Rich.

Rich looked at Yusuf.

Yusuf looked at me.

"CJ, it sounds important, man. It really does, but— that's serious stuff. I'm not sure—" Angel started.

My heart sank to the floor. "Forget about it. You're right. I shouldn't have asked." Maybe I was wrong? Maybe nothing was wrong? The doubts swirled in my head.

I ran down the hall. They shouted after me, but I didn't stop. Tears rushed down my cheeks.

I couldn't let them see it.

As I tried to get home, dozens of people crowded the barricaded entrance to Centennial Olympic Park.

Reporters with microphones, camerapeople, writers scribbling notes down, and even regular folks who might be guests at the park on any given day. Futureland isn't even open on Mondays. No one goes to theme parks on Mondays. Why were they here?

I panicked, trying to figure out how I was going to get past them without being seen. I'd already had a terrible day. I didn't want to talk to anyone. I did a loop around the park, looking for a spot to slip through, but the crowd was thick.

I tried to pull my hoodie up and move through the crowd.

"Watch it, kid," someone barked.

"Wait! That's him!" one of the reporters shouted.

They swarmed. The cameras flashed. Their questions:

"Cameron Walker! How does it feel to be the heir to the Futureland fortune?"

"How much say-so do you have in the park? What's it like to live in the sky?"

"Do you know Iman Sheffield? Have you seen them in the park?"

Sweat dripped down my forehead. "Uh . . . I . . . um . . ." I pushed through to the gate and shouted at the guards to let me in.

The entrance gates cracked open. I rushed in panting. I bent over to catch my breath.

"Your heart is very accelerated, Cameron," came a voice from behind.

I turned around. Dooley's smile greeted me.

"You opened the gate for me. Thanks. Perfect timing," I said, not knowing what else to say. Everything felt different now. The last time I'd seen her, she was crying. Doing something no other rev has ever done. Now she had all this responsibility at the park.

"I noticed your locator coming down the street. I figured you would need some assistance." She gently placed her hands on my shoulder.

I didn't know how to feel or how to treat her. But I missed her.

"Welcome home, Cameron," she said. "Come on. Let's get you up to your room."

I watched her curiously as we walked up the extendo-stair and into Futureland. I hoped she wasn't acting weird. I needed something to be normal.

"Hey, D. Be cool," I said, hoping our command still worked.

"I'm sorry, I don't understand," she replied.

My heart sank.

"You don't remember?"

"Remember what?"

I gulped. Panic shot up my spine.

Dooley turned to face me again, a glint in her eye. "Is something wrong, Cameron?"

"Dooley, I need to ask you something. But it's got to stay a secret. Just between us."

"Yes, Cameron."

"But when I tell you, you can't ever tell anyone else. Okay? That's what *secret* means. Only you know and I know. Can you help me?"

"Of course, Cameron."

I told Dooley the story of opening night and what happened after. She listened to my whole story. "Something is wrong. Have you seen anything strange at Futureland?"

"No, nothing out of the ordinary," she replied.

I tried to study her expression. Could she lie? Was she lying? Revs weren't supposed to be able to do that, but she'd been crying, like, two days ago. Anything was possible now.

Dooley punched the entrance code to the condo.

I checked the wall-o-gram for any to-do tasks and saw nothing. Strange. My parents *always* had a list of things for me to do on Mondays.

I went to my room. Dooley followed. I kept stealing

glances at her over my shoulder. I wanted to tell her not to follow me, but I didn't want to make her suspicious of me.

I plopped down at my desk, riffling through my backpack, tossing aside homework and notebooks and everything else.

"How do you like school, Cameron?" Dooley asked, watching me. The orange of her eyes felt hot and sharp.

I thought about how I'd probably ruined things with my brand-new friends. They probably thought I'd lost it. "Eh, I don't know. Okay, I guess. Things started off all right, but . . . it's weird. It's hard to make friends."

"Are we?"

"Are we what, D?"

"Friends," Dooley said. "*Noun*. A person whom one knows and with whom one has a bond of mutual affection."

I looked at her. She looked puzzled.

"Of course we're friends, D. You're my best friend. Why would you ask that?" The question made me uneasy.

"If we are friends, then you can take me to school with you," she said. "Friends, by my knowledge, often share experiences with one another, spend time together, and go on adventures. I believe that we have done all of these things inside Futureland, Cameron. Like our boat journeys in Future Seas or our moon hops in the Galactic Gallery. Would you agree?"

"Oh . . . you're serious. Yes, yes, I agree—we did all those things. We really are friends. But . . . different kind of friends. You're not supposed to go to school."

Dooley tilted her head. "But I would *like* to go to school, Cameron. And meet more friends."

"I don't go to school to make friends. I go to learn." I held up my notebooks. "You know, class? Learning? That's what all us kids are doing there. While we're at it, we end up making friends. But it can take a while."

"Why do you have other friends . . . but I only have you?" Dooley asked. "You are my only friend. But you have other friends besides me."

"The other revs are your friends, Dooley. Remember?"

"I remember the other revs. But I do not *know* them. Not like I know you."

A chill swept through me. "Dooley . . . Analysis Mode."

She froze.

Weird. Where was all this coming from? These feelings? Maybe my parents gave her a new brain chip, and they didn't mention it to me. Another thing they weren't telling me, added to the list. Maybe this was one of the malfunctions that Uncle Trey was talking about.

My stomach twisted as I checked all of Dooley's stats and saw that everything was operating at standard levels. I hated treating Dooley like a park-rev. Sometimes I had to update her, and it always felt weird to go from her being my friend to her just being another walking, talking body of artificial intelligence.

I clicked my watch, thinking about calling my parents. But . . . I stopped. They probably wouldn't answer anyway. It seemed like nine out of ten times I tried to get their attention about anything these days, they didn't have time. They probably *did* decide to update every rev again after the malfunctions opening night, and Dooley was just glitching.

Yeah, that was it. Had to be. Glitching.

I ran Analysis Mode one more time just to be sure. Dooley was the smartest rev in the park because she had been upgraded so many times for different jobs. But even she had a limit. Mom said if a rev's Reasoning was coded too high, they could end up making decisions that would alter the story lines and interactions Dad wrote for the park. "Predictability means safety," Dad always said.

Dooley's stats were normal again. But why was she

asking these types of questions? Was this why she was crying on opening night, too?

Something was different . . . wrong. But what?

I racked my brain, but I couldn't figure it out. I collapsed on the bed in frustration. Nothing made sense. What would Uncle Trey do? And when would he be back? He could fix anything.

"Resume Standard Mode," I called.

"Hello, Cameron," Dooley greeted.

"Hey, D. Look, I'm sorry I had to do that," I sighed. "Things have just been so confusing lately. I don't feel like I understand anything that's going on."

"What does your intuition say?" Dooley asked.

"Haha! Aw, Dooley. You remember that, huh?"

"The ability to understand something immediately, without the need for conscious reasoning," Dooley rattled off.

"That's it. I have no idea what my intuition says right now. I talked all that talk, and mine isn't even working. It could all just be in my head."

"Perhaps the things in our heads *are* real." Dooley moved closer and patted me on the back.

Another chill ran down my spine. "Dooley?"

Her body jerked, then stiffened. Her eyes stared straight ahead. Her mouth opened and closed like a fish struggling to breathe. "Unable to execute command."

"Dooley, what's wrong? What's going on?" I jumped to my feet. "Activate Safe Mode."

Nothing happened.

I tried again. Panic swirled inside me. Just as I clicked my watch to call my parents, Grandma Ava barreled into my room. "Cameron J. Walker! I have been looking everywhere for you."

I whipped around. "Grandma? What are you doing here?"

"Don't 'huh' me, young man. What are you doing here in this park on a school night"—she looked at Dooley sitting on the bed, face still blank—"with girls in your room?" She put her hands on her hips and tapped her foot.

"Grandma, it's Monday! I always help on Mondays."

"Not this Monday you don't. That was the deal: you spend every school night at the house with me. And where are your parents?! I called and called, but they never came to bring me up. I had to get that nice security man to show me the way. You know, if he was about forty years older . . ,"

"Okay, okay, Grandma," I said. "But could we wait a second? I think there's something wrong with Doo—"

"We don't have no time to wait, Mister Man. It's already past my bedtime, and I've got a kettle on the stove. Pack up. We're headed back to the house, right now."

I rushed to pack up enough of my things for the next few days, and Grandma Ava practically yanked me out of the room. I felt sick to my stomach leaving Dooley malfunctioning on the bed.

Face still blank. Eyes still orange.

And spinning, spinning, spinning . . .

THE HEIST

Saturday, September 12, 2048
11:02 p.m.

I didn't get a chance to go back to Futureland for the rest of the week. I didn't get a chance to see Dooley or check on her. Even though she was reset and told me she was okay, each day away only made me more anxious, more curious, more confused. Aurielle was still at Grandma Ava's house, and I watched her like a hawk. What if Aurielle glitched, too, and tried to hurt Grandma Ava while I was gone?

All the questions took over my mind. I projected a holographic bulletin board from my Futurewatch and pinned messages on it. Made a timeline of the events with virtual index cards, swapping their order over and over, to try to see what made the most sense. I had to figure this out. There had to be something I was missing.

So far, I had a few pieces of *real* evidence.

Glitching revs. Glitching tech. Weird symbol. Weird parents. Missing kid. All happening after we arrived in Atlanta.

I had to solve this thing.

No matter what.

As soon as I was back on Saturday night, I was ready to crack this case and figure it out. Weekend nights when the park was open, my parents would be too busy to track me.

My plan was brilliant, you see. I'd stowed Dooley away in my parents' lab, right with the older revs, before they locked up for the night. She'd disable the security cameras and let me inside so I didn't have to use my login and alert Mom and Dad. We'd search the lab to find about why they were acting so weird. We would be in and out without a trace. Top-tier investigative work.

"Dooley? Dooley, are you ready?" I whispered, testing the microphone Dooley had installed on my Future-vision goggles. If it worked, she'd be able to hear exactly what I'd said, inside her head.

I hid behind a snack stand. Tonight was busier than ever, with little kids sucking on lumi-pops zooming around everywhere.

Dooley to Cam, she called back. Her voice didn't sound out loud. It played inside my head, for only me

147

to hear. Dooley's updates to the Future-vision goggles worked perfectly. *Everything is ready, over.*

"Great." I swiped screens on my watch. "My parents are still in the Galactic Gallery. We only have about forty-five minutes to get everything."

Ready when you are, she replied.

"See you in ten."

I speed-walked down the Futureland paths, hustling to get back to the condo to enter the lab from there.

"CJ!"

I stopped in my tracks.

I spun around. It was Yusuf, out of breath and wearing a black hoodie and sneakers.

"Yusuf? Uh—what—what's going on? Are you okay?" I asked.

"Are *you* okay?" he asked. "You haven't been answering your phone. And you barely talked to us all week at school. I came to check on you. Long shot trying to find you with all these people here, but . . . I figured where else would you be?"

"Oh . . . yeah." I fidgeted. I'd really messed things up.

Nerves rushed into my stomach, right as Dooley's voice came through my goggles again. I couldn't fix this right now. "Yusuf, I just—I just got some stuff to handle. But we'll talk later, okay?"

"Sounds serious. Like you could use some help,"

he replied. "And I'm really sorry we couldn't help you at first. I didn't know what to say or do. No one has really needed my help like that before. But I can help you now."

My heart started to beat faster, and my eyes widened. "You sure?" I wanted to be hopeful, even though making new friends was complicated.

"Positive," he said.

I looked at my watch, and my brain started to buzz. "Okay, okay. But we've got to move fast. Let's go!"

I took Yusuf back to the condo with me. I tried my best to keep him focused on the mission and not all the cool gadgets he hadn't seen before. I took him to my room and handed him my tablet.

"Okay, so I need your eyes glued to this." I pointed at the screen and showed him how to use it. "See those little glowing things. They're locators. I need you to watch the ones for my parents."

"Cool." He held it up.

"I need to know if they decide to leave the Galactic Gallery and head back here. If they do, use this watch. It'll send me a message." I put last season's Futurewatch on his wrist. "I'll be back."

"I got it. Won't let you down." He smiled.

We piled into the Future Trek tree house, spreading the papers all over the floor to analyze. I tried to calm down and look for clues.

"This place is dope." Yusuf gazed all around at the hanging orchids and these really pretty red flowers that Uncle Trey called lobster claws.

"It's one of my favorites," I said, hoping being here would help me focus. "Y'all finding anything good?"

"Hard to tell." Yusuf held up a page. "I don't know what most of this stuff means."

"We've only got about fifteen minutes before midnight," Dooley said.

Yusuf looked at the tablet. "Dr. Walker and Mr. Walker have their locators off. What should we do, Cam?"

I gulped. *Family business is family business.* I knew I shouldn't go into detail about the inner workings of the park. I'd have to betray one of the Walker Ways of Living.

"I don't know how much I can explain. It's like . . . it's family business."

"No offense, Cam," Yusuf said, "but this feels bigger

than family business now. I promise you can trust me. I can keep secrets."

Maybe he was right. Ever since I'd come to Atlanta, I'd been so scared about not fitting in. Then, since everything started happening with the park, I'd been worried about my parents and worried about Future-land. But my friends were the answer. Yusuf was here, bringing my school world into my home world and trying to help make both better. I could trust him with this information. Other than Dooley, he might have been the only one I *could* trust.

I explained the park technology, system updates, and how the revs go through different upgrades as we kept riffling through papers.

"Hey, what's this?" Yusuf waved the piece of paper in the air.

"Cameron——" Dooley started.

"Hold on, D. What's that, Yusuf?" I grabbed it. "Looks like one of my parents' meeting reports. The ones with investors and other businesspeople who want to be involved with the park."

"What is A-D-R-C?" he asked.

I scanned the document quickly to see if the acronym was spelled out anywhere.

" 'The Atlanta Disuse and Redevelopment Corporation,' " I read. "Ever heard of it?"

"Wait, yes." Yusuf stared at the paper. "Earl's foster dad—I think he works there. He came on career day last year. They take down old buildings in the city and build up new, fancy ones."

"That's exactly what this paper says," I told him.

"Cameron—" Dooley started again.

"What do they have to do with anything?" Yusuf looked at me.

"I'm not sure," I replied. "But looks like somebody named Blaise Southmore from the ADRC came to the last Futureland business meeting. Heard of him?"

Where had I seen that name before?

"Nope, but I'll ask Earl. Maybe he can find out more for us. I can check the library, too. Maybe he's in the newspapers or magazines."

"Great! Okay. We've got a clue. Let's take these papers—"

"CAMERON!" Dooley shouted, startling Yusuf and me.

"What, Dooley?! Jeez," I said.

"It's midnight."

The door to the tree house swung open. Wind rushed in, sending the papers in a thousand directions. Two figures stood in the entrance.

Yusuf crouched low. Dooley stayed put.

I froze in fear.

The figures stepped into the dim light of the tree house. One, tall, with a beehive of locs atop her head. One, squatty and stout, his broad shoulders taking up more than half of the doorway.

"Mom? Dad?"

A creepy smile spread across their faces. Their eyes bore into me. They looked like my parents.

But for a moment, I wasn't quite sure. A cold shiver shot up my spine.

"Hi, Cam-Cam," Mom said, her voice raspy. "Hi, Cam's friend. Care for a midnight snack?"

12

A MIDNIGHT SNACK

Sunday, September 13, 2048
12:03 a.m.

A midnight snack?" I asked, confused.

Dad did a weird twitch with his neck, then smiled again. "Why, yes. We have Astromilk and star-cookies in the condo," he said.

"Very yummy," Mom chimed in.

"I think everyone would love them," Dad said.

"Very yummy," Mom added again.

Yusuf and I looked at each other.

I swallowed. "Um, okay?"

"Splendid," Mom said. "We will see you there in ten minutes. Dooley, come with us." She and Dad stepped backward, in unison, one step at a time until they were out of the door and gone from the tree house.

I couldn't speak. Goose bumps covered me from head to toe. I didn't know what to do.

Dooley stood, then looked at me. Her eyes softened. She looked sad, like she was about to cry again. Like opening night.

"CJ . . . that was . . ." Yusuf put his hands on his head, stunned.

My mind raced. "They didn't . . . they didn't say anything about the park closing. Like how I should have been helping. Or all these papers around. Or you being here! They . . . they were just acting so . . ."

"Weird!" Yusuf finished my sentence.

Yusuf and I hustled the papers, documents, and tablets back into our packs. Yusuf promised he would ask Earl about ADRC to see what he could find out. I tried to get him to leave, but he insisted on staying for the snack.

"This is really strange, CJ," he said. "I've already stretched curfew. I can stretch it a little more. I'm scared to leave you alone."

I felt grateful to him as we walked to the condo. I wouldn't have to face them by myself.

When Yusuf and I got to the kitchen, Dooley was pulling the star-cookies out of the oven. She kept her head down and didn't look us in the eye. My parents sat next to one another on the same side of the table, not speaking.

They just looked at us. Smiling.

Not smiling like they were happy to see us, like . . . they had a secret.

Dooley set the cookies in the middle of the table and sat down with us. Cinnamon-swirling Astromilk and star-shaped cookies with chocolate chips. Our chef-rev Alejandro's special recipe. Nobody moved.

Yusuf and I traded glances.

"Uh . . . you have a lovely home, Dr. and Mr. Walker," Yusuf said. "Thank you for the cookies."

"No problem, young man," Mom said. "What is your name again?"

"Yusuf. I go to school with CJ—uh, with Cameron."

"So nice to meet you . . . Yusuf," Dad replied.

Just then, I heard the toilet flush in the hall bathroom. I spun around in my chair, then back to my parents.

"Is . . . is somebody here?" I asked.

"Ohhhh, yes." Mom grinned, giggling. "We forgot to mention. Someone will be joining us for Astromilk and star-cookies. I guess we *all* invited secret company over tonight, huh?" She winked.

I swallowed. "Who would be here so late at night?"

Slow, careful steps sounded from the hallway as

we all turned to watch. After a moment, a tall white man—the palest I'd ever seen—stepped into view. His hair was so blond, it was almost white, and he had it gelled back and parted to one side with lines more perfect than the ones in geometry class. He had on a dark suit and big, shiny rings on his fingers. He stepped into the dining room with us, close enough for me to make out his blue-gray eyes and yellow teeth.

I startled. The memory of his face rushed through me. I'd seen him before. Last week, actually. The first time Dooley walked me to school, one of the protesters had a sign with his face on it.

"Well, good evenin', y'all. And howdy, young man. You must be Cameron." He stretched my name out to Cam-uh-rin with his super-thick southern accent. He smiled his gross smile and stuck his hand out for me to shake it.

I sat still, looking back and forth between him and my parents.

"Aw, don't be shy," he continued. "I promised I washed my hands real good." He let out a hacking laugh that sounded more like a cough. I put a shaky hand out, and he grabbed it and squeezed it tight. "Now, I've already made Dooley's acquaintance, but who is our other young friend here tonight?"

"That would be . . . Yusuf, Cameron's new friend from school," Mom said.

"Simply delightful." He grinned again. "Happy to have you join us, Yusuf. Have you had Futureland's famous Astromilk and star-cookies before? I've heard marvelous things about them."

Yusuf tapped his foot under the table. "Um. No, sir. First time."

"Mine, too." The man crunched on a cookie and took a slurp of milk. "Mmm-mm. Well, the stories are true. Go ahead, try one."

Yusuf and I picked up cookies and nibbled at them. My parents kept sitting, smiling, with their hands in their laps.

"Um, who are you?" I asked.

"I'm sorry?" the man said.

"You didn't introduce yourself."

"Oh, heavens. Pardon me, how rude," he replied.

"No, no. That is our fault," Dad said. "Cameron, Yusuf—this is Mr. Blaise Southmore."

My stomach backflipped. I tried to keep a straight face, but I could feel Yusuf's eyes on me. *The* Blaise Southmore? From the papers we took from Dad's lab?

What was he doing here? And at this time of night?

"Mr. Southmore was accompanying us around the control center as we worked on some new settings for the park," Mom said. "He took time out of his busy schedule to come after work and see how we run things around here."

"The pleasure was truly all mine. What a fantastic park you all have here. You should be very proud of it. And these, uh, what do you call 'em—revs? Simply delightful. I mean, I wish I could take 'em all home with me. Imagine that—revs in the home. It would make life *so* much easier," Southmore said.

I frowned. I tried to read my parents' expressions for some clues. We all could communicate with little facial expressions and shifts in energy that we learned from each other over the years.

But looking at them across the table, I couldn't tell a thing.

They just kept grinning. Hands in their laps.

I studied their faces, their posture. They were . . . stiff. Tense. They looked like Earl in class when the teacher asked him to answer a question, but he hadn't done the homework. Like they didn't quite know what to say, but they had to pretend everything was okay. Something was going on with this Southmore guy, and whatever it was—it wasn't good.

Why would they be inviting someone like this to the control center? I couldn't remember a single time in all of Futureland history where an outsider got to go up there. Especially not one like this, who seemed so . . . well . . . scary.

"Mr. Southmore is very influential in the Atlanta community, Cam-Cam," Mom said. "He leads a team of investors that is willing to help Futureland become the best it's ever been."

"Huh?" I said. "But Futureland is already the best it's ever been. You and Dad said so yourselves when we were first landed here. Opening night went great. Why do we need *him*?"

"Mind your manners." My mom's soft voice turned into a raspy growl, and her eyes were like darts.

"I have some very big visions for Futureland," Southmore added. "The park is wonderful as is— you're right. I wouldn't be trying to *change* things. Just . . . enhance them. Futureland is big. But I'm thinking even bigger. This city is full of possibilities."

"But y'all said you didn't want investors and people digging around in our business," I said, trying to keep the whine out of my voice. I knew I was pushing my luck, but I couldn't help it. "You said that everybody wanted a piece of Futureland and that you wanted to protect it. That you built it from the ground up and you wouldn't let it get ruined!" I was gasping now, throwing out everything I could remember about our conversations, hoping even one little piece of information would jog my parents' memories and snap them out of this trance.

They sat still, facing me, and for a moment, the smiles disappeared. They looked puzzled, even trading glances with each other. But just as quickly as the new expressions came, they left, and the grins returned. My mom spoke first.

"Well, then. Maybe we did say that. But . . . things are different now. We have changed our minds. We're very excited about working with Mr. Southmore and his team."

"And I'm excited to work with you all," Southmore added. "Though, I'm afraid I may have overstayed my welcome for the night. I'll be on my way. Yusuf, is it? Would you like a ride home?"

"Uhhh—" Yusuf flinched.

"No, he's good. I already called him a ride." I tapped my Futurewatch.

I hadn't, but I didn't want him to be alone with that guy.

"Right, then," Southmore replied. "Well, Cam-uh-rin, my office is east of the city, pretty close to your school. Feel free to stop by anytime to chat. Your parents told me your Futureland knowledge is second to none." He handed me a business card. "Dooley, would you mind accompanying me down to the ground? I can find my way from there."

"My pleasure, Mr. Southmore," Dooley murmured.

Southmore left, and my parents got up from the table. Alejandro started clearing the dishes. Yusuf and I agreed to meet at school to talk about everything that had happened. After Dooley dropped Southmore off, she came back to escort Yusuf to the ground to catch the ride I'd called.

I tried to find my parents to ask them about Southmore, but I couldn't find them. Again.

Not in their bedroom. Not in the lab. Locators off.

They didn't even say good night.

I walked into my room and turned the business card over in my hand. It had the names *Blaise Southmore* and *ADRC* on it in fancy, shiny ink. Contact information, too. And underneath it all, a company logo, shining just as bright.

A glossy circle, with a rectangle inside of it.

INTERVIEW OUTPUT REPORT 0005

Date: 09-14-2048

Location: ADRC HQ

Interviewer: Unlogged

Subject: A4-030-1

INTERVIEWER: What have you done with the kid?

A4-030-1: I finished the task. They will not be found.

INTERVIEWER: Great. Now, on to the next task.

A4-030-1: I cannot fix the controls in the park how you want. You'll have to do it yourself.

INTERVIEWER: Do it myself? Who is working for who here?

A4-030-1: [*microphone registered silence*]

INTERVIEWER: Fine. I'll figure it out. Does Cameron suspect anything?

A4-030-1: No. Not yet.

INTERVIEWER: Not yet?

A4-030-1: He's very smart. It's only a matter of time. He'll know something is wrong.

INTERVIEWER: It's your job to make sure he doesn't figure out *what* is wrong.

A4-030-1: I'll try. This is hard for me.

INTERVIEWER: Boo-hoo. Get the job done. We'll be watching.

From: Atlanta Eastside District Schools
To: All Parents
Subj: Details for Iman Sheffield
September 14, 2048, at 7:32 a.m.

IMAN SHEFFIELD
Height: 5'5"
Weight: 130 lbs.
Hair: Brown
Eyes: Brown

It is with great concern that we write to inform you all that there have been <u>no</u> leads as to the disappearance of Eastside Middle School 8th grader

Iman Sheffield. Iman was last seen on 9/5/2048, leaving the Futureland theme park in downtown Atlanta.

Iman's mother, Dana, has been working with our school system to send out information that may help identify Iman.

Dana will be coordinating a community search and safety group for all who are interested in pitching in. Please respond to this email if you are willing to get involved.

Stay safe.

—Eastside Middle School Administration

13

PRETEND PARENTS

Monday, September 14, 2048
5:30 p.m.

investigated all day Sunday. During my park rounds, I saw more and more ADRC logos hidden in places—drawn in the dirt, carved into the sides of buildings. Revs didn't respond to commands—they huddled together, mumbling among themselves . . . almost like they were sharing secrets. Their eyes stopped glowing orange when they processed. I thought it was just the park lights at first, but no—they were glowing red.

I still hadn't heard from Uncle Trey. Nobody had seen or heard from Iman Sheffield. And my parents . . . It made my heart hurt to think about them. I missed the way things were before. Mom and Dad were still acting creepy. Was I the only one noticing all the weird things going on?

I had at least figured out one thing, and I was preeetty sure I had the right idea. That Southmore guy *must* have something to do with the malfunctioning revs and technology around Futureland. Why else would the logo for his company be showing up every time something went haywire?

But why? What could Southmore gain from busting up Futureland tech? Was he looking for something specific or just trying to make trouble?

After nagging the resistance out of Grandma Ava, I got permission to come to Futureland after school to help with the off-day calibrations in the park. My parents' locators were in the Word Locus, so I called a Jet-Blur pod to pick me up. It cruised to a stop on the park terrace, and I hopped in. As I was buckling up, a message from Yusuf emerged on my watch's hologram.

I listened: *"Took all weekend of bugging Earl, but he finally asked his foster dad more about ADRC. It's not just buying old buildings and building fancy ones. It's any and everything with technology. They take old computers, phones, tablets—anything. He says they make a lot of money doing it. He says they'd take over all of Atlanta if they could."*

I sent him a message back: "Good info. Thanks. I'll check in later."

The Jet-Blur pod whizzed and swerved around all the destinies until it passed through the entrance to the Word Locus.

As the pod descended, the air filled with the scent of fresh paper and wet ink. We soared over trees made totally of books—from the trunks to the branches to the leaves, and winding trails that led to the Tree Tower—a giant library with hanging bookshelves swaying in the breeze.

The pod dropped me at the bottom of the tower. I slowly made my way up the winding staircase. At the top, the tree divided into three different peaks, each one a library with different kinds of books inside. I looked up at three pulsing signs: ADVENTURE, FANTASY, and HORROR. All a guest had to do was open up their favorite book and be transported to a virtual-reality version of it.

I scanned for my parents. I knew they were rotating the settings today. Changing the world genres to give guests some new experiences.

"Hey, Mom. Hey, Dad," I called out.

"In here," I heard my dad yell from an upstairs room.

I took careful steps. I balled my fists and tried to calm down. I had to pretend nothing was wrong. I had to ask some questions to figure out what was wrong with them and get to the bottom of all these weird behaviors. Detective Cam was on the case.

I climbed to the top of the tower and found my parents in the Adventure peak.

My dad turned around slowly, his smile widening. "Hey there, Little Man. Thanks for coming. We didn't expect you to arrive so early. We thought you might be completing your homework."

"Yeah, I finished it during my break period. I wanted to be here for this. *Always make time for each other,* right?"

"I'm sorry?" Dad's nose scrunched.

I scrunched mine up in return. "You know. Walker Way of Living number one. *Always make time for each other.*"

My stomach tightened.

"Oh, yes, yes, of course. Thank you for making time. You can help your mother on that side. She's recoding some of the virtual realities based on new stories I've chosen."

I walked over to her, my footsteps echoing on the shiny tile floors of the great hall of books. Ceiling-high windows flooded the room with natural light as the entire peak rocked gently back and forth in the never-ending breeze of the Word Locus.

I peered through the window, spotting one of the hanging bookshelves in full swing.

"What's up, Mom? I missed you." I leaned in for a hug.

Mom awkwardly put her hands on my shoulders as I squeezed her.

"How can I help?" I asked.

She turned back to her tablet. "Please hand me those books, one by one. They have codes on them. I'm putting them into the system."

As I handed her each book, she typed something into her tablet and then set the books aside.

"Hey, Mom? Is Uncle Trey still on vacation?" I asked.

"Hmm. Yes. Vacation. He's been on vacation for quite some time, hasn't he? I suppose it's time he stopped being lazy and came back to work."

I paused with a book in my hand. "Mom? Are you feeling okay?"

"I feel great, Little Man. Why do you ask?"

"Well, you never say stuff like that about Uncle Trey. He's not lazy. He works really hard around here. Are you mad at him or something?"

I noticed it again—that weird pause before answering that my parents had started doing lately. Almost like they were . . . processing.

"Oh. Ha, ha. No, no. I'm not mad at him. Just a little joke, is all," she said finally.

"Right."

Mom grabbed the last few books from me all at once.

"Thanks for your help. Why don't you go get washed up for dinner? Your father and I will meet you downstairs in the condo."

"Yeah, all right," I grumbled. "Thanks for letting me help out in your favorite park destiny." I gazed at Mom, anticipating her response.

"No problem, Little Man."

I bolted back down the stairs with steps made out of books all the way to the bottom of the massive tree trunk. I checked my watch for Dooley's locator. Off. We'd have to catch up later.

I had a new plan.

The dinner table was silent. My parents sat neatly, hands folded in their laps, barely touching their food. I tried to chat with them but got one-word answers. Walker family dinners were usually loud and full of jokes.

I tried to pretend everything was fine, even though my heart was beating a mile a minute and sweat dripped down my back. I let my parents go through the usual routine. Tucking me into bed and saying good night.

"We hope you have a restful sleep, Cam," they said together.

"Thanks," I replied. "So you won't need my help tomorrow, right? I'll go back to Grandma Ava's after school?"

Mom frowned. "Why would you do that?"

"Uh. That's what we've been doing. Y'all wanted me to spend weeknights there so I could adjust to living on the ground and have time to do my homework. Oh, and Grandma Ava said y'all have to come once a week for dinner, too."

"Hmm," Dad said. "We changed our minds. You can come to Futureland every day after school. I'm sure everything will be fine."

"What about Grandma Ava?" I asked.

"Oh, I'll let her know," Mom replied. "She'll just have to understand."

My pulse quickened. "Okay. Hey, Mom and Dad?" They smiled.

"What ever happened to that gorilla in Future

Trek? The one that was having issues when we first got to Atlanta?"

Mom and Dad exchanged glances, silent for a moment.

"Ah, yes. I believe Trey was able to complete repairs on it before his vacation started," Dad said. "But you shouldn't worry about those things."

"Oh. Uncle Trey told me he didn't fix it," I lied, testing him. I hadn't talked to Uncle Trey at all about the gorilla repairs.

"No! He . . . couldn't figure it out. I am the one who fixed it," Mom insisted.

I gulped. They were lying. "Oh, okay. Did you ever figure out exactly what was wrong?"

Mom hesitated. "Yes . . . but it's much too complicated for you to understand. Besides, who wants to talk about a gross gorilla-rev before bedtime?"

My heart thundered, and my pulse raced in my ears. I took a deep breath. *Keep pretending,* I told myself.

"Is everything okay, Cam?" Mom asked, cocking her head to the side.

"It's fine, and you're right. Well, thanks anyway. Revs could be really dangerous if they just started malfunctioning all over the place . . . don't you think?" My breath caught. "I'm glad we could *Activate Temporary Safe Mode* when we went to check on it. . . ."

At the sound of the command, both of my parents' faces froze in place, their newly adopted smiles perfectly crooked. Their expressions went blank.

It was only a split-second delay. Seriously, if I would have blinked, I would have missed it. But I didn't blink. And now I had all the information I needed.

My heart pounded so hard, it threatened to give out.

"That's a great point, Cameron," Mom said. "You're so smart. Time to get some rest. Good night." She flicked off the light, and she and Dad left the room.

I burrowed deep under the covers and projected my journal app from my Futurewatch.

Clue #1: My real dad would never forget the Walker Ways of Living. Especially not the very first one.

Clue #2: Since when did my parents start calling me Little Man? It's always been Big Man.

Clue #3: My real mom doesn't have a favorite park destiny. She doesn't play favorites.

Clue #4: This Mom hasn't squeezed me or kissed my forehead one time since my parents started acting all weird. Sure, I hate it, but it's how she shows her love. She wouldn't just stop.

All these clues could only lead to one possible explanation. My hands quivered as the truth bubbled up.

Those people . . . are not my parents.

They're running the park, they're meeting investors, and they're feeding me dinner.

But they're not my mom and dad.

My mom and dad are missing.

And I think . . . I think they've been replaced with revs.

14

NOT A REV ANYMORE

Tuesday, September 15, 2048
7:00 p.m.

I told Yusuf to meet me after school. That it was an emergency. I barely made it out of the building. My focus was all over the place. Panic every two seconds. The realization from last night pouring over me every time I stopped focusing on classwork.

I burst out the school's front doors as soon as the last bell rang. Yusuf was waiting for me by the tree on the school's front lawn.

I rushed up to him. "I've got so much to tell you."

"Not here," Yusuf said. "Let's go."

I followed him. "Where are we going?"

"You'll see."

We walked to a neighborhood a few streets over.

The houses soared over us, beautiful lawns and fancy cars. Yusuf walked up the biggest driveway and rang the bell.

Rich answered the door. "Took y'all long enough."

"What are we doing here?" I asked, confused.

"I said you'll see!" Yusuf repeated.

We chased Rich up his front staircase and into his huge bedroom. The whole crew was there. Earl stuffing his face and Angel playing video games on the flat-screen TV. Neon floor lights made everything green, and a remote-controlled drone flew overhead.

You'd think Rich was the one whose parents owned Futureland.

"Hey, Cam!" they each shouted.

"What's going on?" I wrung my hands in my lap, my pulse speeding up.

Angel turned the game off, and Earl stopped eating. They all turned to face me.

"Yusuf told us what was going on," Angel said. "With the park and everything. So we're going to help you."

My heartbeat skipped.

"We should've helped you from the start," Earl said.

"We didn't realize it was so . . . dire," Angel added.

"We decided as a group." Earl got super serious and made eye contact with me. "Nobody should have to face something like this alone. And we trust Yusuf. If he says it's a big deal—then it's a big deal."

"Wah-wah, blah, blah. You still want help with the investigation, or whatever you called it? Eastside Middle's favorite crew of misfits, at your service," Rich announced.

"Wait, wait, wait—are y'all for real?" I said.

"No jokes," Yusuf said. "We're your friends. We've got your back."

A weight slid off me. Tears welled up in my eyes. I bit my bottom lip to keep from crying.

I jumped to my feet and grabbed Rich—he was the closest to me—and gave him a big hug.

"Ew, what are you doing, new kid?!"

"Thanks so much, man," I sniffled.

The rest of the crew gathered around and made one big ball of a group hug with Rich at the middle. He wasn't strong enough to shake the four of us off. Finally, he gave in, and we all laughed.

"Now, tell us everything," Angel commanded.

I started from the top, detailing every part of my investigation and observations to my friends. I felt like a detective bringing in others onto the case, getting everyone up to speed. The documents Yusuf and I got were in my backpack, and I took them out and passed them around.

"You're kidding, right, CJ? Your parents? Revs? No way." Earl's eyes were so wide, I thought they might fall out of his head.

Angel looked at me. "But they're your parents. How can they be revs? They're taking care of you, right? Feeding you, sending you to school. How could a rev do that?"

"They *were* super weird during that snack," Yusuf said.

I kept going. "The main thing in a rev's brain is a story line. Revs can do anything as long as they have the right script. My parents' whole lives are in Futureland—all their personal information, their journals, their computers. If somebody wanted to make rev versions of my parents . . . they'd have all the information they could need."

"Who would want to do something like that?" Rich looked confused.

"I don't know." I shook my head. "I thought maybe that Blaise Southmore guy. He seems pretty suspicious."

"He's definitely creepy," Yusuf added. "But he's already rich. What would he want with Futureland? What would he do with a park for kids?"

He had a point. Ugh, maybe I had the wrong lead.

"I'm not really sure," I admitted. "But I've been

thinking." I projected my bulletin board and notepad into the air from my Futurewatch to share my notes.

"Cool," Rich said. "I need a watch like that."

"I'll get you one, but focus." I turned back to the projection of my notes. "So the Futureland tech has been glitching. Each time, *this* symbol came up." I pointed to the circle with the rectangle inside. "That's—"

"The logo for my dad's company." Earl jumped up.

"Exactly. The same company that Southmore owns. So I'm pretty sure he's been trying to hack our tech remotely. At first I wasn't sure why. But then I remembered something he said about wishing he could take revs home with him. Earl, I was thinking maybe he wanted to use ARDC to maybe collect some revs for his own use. What do you think?" I asked.

"But that company is all about taking old things and making them new. Or totally replacing old things with new ones. Futureland is the newest, best tech there is. I don't know how Southmore or ADRC would use the park . . . unless . . ." Earl started to pace. "Unless he wants to make it *look* like the revs are old and broken. Then it would be like you said, CJ. He could take them for himself. I'm just not sure what he'd do with them."

"Yeah, yeah." I nodded. "I don't know, either."

"He should still be on the suspect list," Angel chimed in.

Everyone nodded in approval.

"Any other ideas for suspects?" I asked.

"Iman Sheffield is still missing. It's barely in the news anymore. All the teachers around school try to make us keep hush about it. Maybe these cases are related," Yusuf said.

"No way, Yusuf," Rich argued. "Kids go missing in Atlanta all the time."

"Mm-hmm. Like in the eighties. A *bunch* of kids went missing in the eighties," Earl said. "We learned about it in history class. Big scandal. Police waited way too long to help."

"Sure, but how often do kids go missing after visiting Futureland?" Angel pressed.

They all turned to look at me.

"I . . . I can't ever remember that happening." My stomach coiled.

"Hmm. Okay. Well, write that down, too. I'll ask my mom if she's heard anything else about Iman. She's a receptionist at the Justice Center downtown," Rich said.

Yusuf put his hand up like he was in school. Everyone turned to face him. "CJ, back to the rev thing— let's just say for a moment that some revs have replaced your parents. Then where are your real parents? Do you think they could be in danger?"

"Yeah. I've been trying not to think about that. I wouldn't even know where to start looking for them if they were missing. I don't know anything about Atlanta. They could be anywhere," I said.

Yusuf frowned. "Well, how would you know if your parents *are* revs? How can you tell the difference between a human and a rev?"

"Well . . . it's hard. But there are a few ways. Revs have a fluid inside them—kinda like blood—but it's orange. It helps them operate."

"So we have to open up a rev just to be sure?" Earl looked grossed out.

"Sounds risky. What other ways?" Angel asked.

"Hmm. There used to be things that revs didn't know. That they couldn't understand. Like secrets. Or some jokes. But . . . my dad's been working on giving them better understanding, less confusion. Ugh, so I guess that's not the best way to tell, either, huh?"

"Nope," Rich said.

"Come on, CJ. Think hard." Yusuf put his hand on my shoulder. "There has to be at least *one* thing we can use. One way to know for sure if your parents are humans or revs."

The room went quiet for a moment while I racked my brain. I looked around the room at my friends. Angel flipping through the playlist. Yusuf spinning his basketball on his fingers. Rich playing video games. Earl messily eating his snacks and wiping the chocolate off his face.

Wait. That's it.

"The face!" I jumped up and ran over to Earl, grabbing his shoulders and bringing his face close to mine. "Revs can't touch faces. They can't touch human faces. They can't touch another rev's face. There was no way to code it. My parents tried and tried to fix the glitch, but that kind of affection is too human. My dad was *just* telling me that he still couldn't figure it out, even with the new revs."

"So if your rev parents tried to touch your face and couldn't . . . ," Yusuf started.

"Or if they *avoided* touching my face—like my mom did when I hugged her in the Word Locus. She always squeezes me tight and kisses my forehead. But she hasn't done it in so long." I paced the room like a madman.

The comm-box on Rich's nightstand buzzed. "What, Pierre?" he barked. "I'm with my friends."

"Apologies, Mister Rich. We have a visitor here for one of your guests. A Miss Dooley here to see Mr. Cameron. Should I send her up?"

The whole crew turned to look at me.

"Is Dooley here to help with the case?" Earl asked.

"I—I don't know," I confessed. "I didn't know she was coming. Maybe I should go down and meet her."

"You need backup?" Yusuf said.

"Nah, I got this. It's Dooley, and"—I took a deep breath—"just so you all know . . . she's a rev, too, and my best friend."

Rich looked shocked as I darted out of the room.

"Hey, do you need these?" Rich called after me, holding out the goggles. I waved him off.

I made my way downstairs and down the pathway to the end of Rich's driveway. I looked over my shoulder to the window of the room I had just come from and saw a break in the blinds. One of my friends was peeking out at me. A light rain started drizzling on Dooley and me as we stood in the driveway.

"Dooley. How'd you know where I was?" I asked.

Dooley looked strange. Her eyes were spinning wildly. "Cam, I have something important to tell you."

A pit burned in my stomach. Was she malfunctioning again? "What's up, D?"

"You've got to stop investigating Blaise Southmore and ADRC."

Her words made me stumble backward. "What? How do you know— What do you mean? Dooley—"

"No, Cam. Just stop. Don't say anything else. You have to stop. Please. Listen to me. No more snooping around and searching. It's for your own good."

I shook my head. "I don't understand."

"I'm sorry, Cam."

"How are you talking to me like this? Analysis Mode."

"Now's not the time for analysis, Cam. I can't explain what's going on. But you need to be careful. You, your friends, your uncle Trey. You're all in grave danger."

I felt my chest tighten up like an elastic band. My head got dizzy. Did Dooley just reject a command? What did she mean we were in danger?

Dooley looked me squarely in the eye. "I can't help you and your friends, Cam. I wish I could, but I can't. I've got my own mission I have to take care of. I'm sorry."

Before I could get another word out, she turned to walk down the street. The rain started to pour as I watched Dooley's afro-puffs get smaller in the distance.

"But, Dooley!" I called after her. "How? How did you— You're a rev!"

Dooley turned in the middle of the street and faced

me once more, the rain coming down all around her. A rumble of thunder felt like it shook the pavement, and a bolt of lightning flashed behind Dooley, giving her a glow for a brief second. She remained still, looking straight through me.

"I'm not a rev, Cam. Not anymore."

CAN'T GET ENOUGH OF
FUTURELAND?
Hotlanta's Hottest New Attraction?
Future-rific. The world's most innovative theme park is here to stay.
Porting in Atlanta for the rest of 2048!
Bring a friend and enjoy the fun!
Interested in joining the Futureland Board of Investors? Click the link for more details on setting up a tour and business meeting.

15

ALL IN MY MIND

Saturday, September 19, 2048
1:00 p.m.

D ooley's words—*I'm not a rev anymore*—played
over and over in my head for days. And her warning. I was in danger. And my other friends, too.

I had no idea what to do.

It all felt too big for me to handle. Maybe I wasn't
the detective I thought I was.

Maybe this was all a really bad dream. Maybe if I
just pretended that nothing was wrong, then all the
bad things would go away.

Maybe. But probably not.

I missed my family more than ever. My parents—
the real ones—and Uncle Trey, and Dooley. Nothing
had been normal since we got to Atlanta. We used to
all be one tight unit. But now . . . all the people I loved

the most were getting farther and farther away from me. And I couldn't figure out what was happening.

Everything was a blur. School was still a mess. Yusuf walked me to class most of the time, and when he couldn't, Angel did, shaking her fist at every kid that got too close to us. I found notes in my locker begging me for advance Future Passes, for extra tickets, and to get off the waitlist. Even Ms. Green asked me to stay after homeroom to talk about an assignment, just to ask how she could score some tickets for her nieces and nephews. I walked through the halls, shoulders drooping, with big bags under my eyes. Exhausted.

As much as I tried to pretend things were normal, I couldn't. I hated my pretend parents and wanted my real ones back. Forgetting simple things, bringing new events to the park, and smiling. Always smiling, with their hands in their laps.

I didn't know how to fix everything before someone got hurt.

I burrowed in my room, barricading my desk in front of the door in case the pretend parents tried to come in.

My watch vibrated. Angel was calling. I clicked the button. A projection of her illuminated. "Hey, CJ!"

"Hey," I mumbled back.

"I'm about to text you something. Earl found out

more about ADRC," Angel said. "He's quite the little researcher. Who knew?"

"I'll take a look, then—" I paused. The noise of footsteps echoed from the hall. "I gotta go."

"Call me back later," she said before I hung up.

A knock pounded the door. "Cam?"

Mom's voice. Well, pretend Mom.

"Yes?" I replied, bracing.

"I need you dressed and ready. Meet us at the Guest Hub. We have an announcement."

"Okay," I replied, then waited to hear the unnaturally perfect sound of her footsteps walking away.

What kind of announcement? I had the feeling this wasn't going to be good.

I got up and headed to the Guest Hub at the park entrance. Dread filled me. What could this be? The Millennium Marketplace band rushed out, stepping to the beat, drumming and blowing their horns, urging the entire crowd to sway and clap with them. Even some of the dancers from the Future Theater came with them. For about two minutes, it was one big party. Until *he* walked out.

Blaise Southmore.

Southmore stepped onto the platform, tapping his foot and shaking his arms around, totally missing the beat, grinning greedily and smiling out into the crowd. He had on the same style suit as before, same slick hairstyle, and same ghostly appearance as the last time I'd seen him.

But what was he doing here?

The music lowered, and my pretend parents came out onto the stage, dressed in their official Futureland jumpsuits and lapel pins.

"Welcome, all! Thank you so much for joining us on this special occasion. We have some very exciting news." My mom looked over at my dad.

"Yes, yes, we do! Since we've landed in Atlanta, you all have showed us so much support, and we've been pushing our own boundaries to imagine how the park can be even greater than we ever dreamed. We believe we've found a way," Dad said.

"None of it would be possible without the help of one man. . . ." Mom raised her hands in the air.

No.

"One man who has proved himself a true friend . . ."

No. No.

"A man who loves Futureland just as much as we do. We'd like to formally introduce you all to the new president of our Board of Investors . . . Mr. Blaise Southmore!"

My stomach plummeted.

"Thank you, Stacy, J. B.," Southmore said. "This is such a great honor. How y'all doing out there?" He smiled. "Y'all enjoy that fabulous music? Just makes you want to cut a rug, doesn't it?"

People in the crowd laughed. Not everybody. But some.

"Well, I'm simply delighted to accept this role. I have grand plans to bridge the gap between Futureland and the city of Atlanta. We will work together, as one, to create something the world has never seen."

The cheers from the crowd were so loud, my head started to spin.

How could my parents let this happen?

I turned to leave the platform and felt . . . uneasy. But then anxiety shot through me.

Like eyes were on me.

I whipped around and peered through the crowd. I found a pair of eyes staring back at me. A teenage girl with two long pigtails falling over her shoulders and a ball cap pulled low. I started making my way to her through the crowd, but she started moving, too. By the time I got to where I had first seen her, she was gone.

Was she a Watcher or a human? Could all this be a coincidence?

What did it say that I couldn't tell the difference anymore?

"I reckon you were in the park with all that hoopla today, huh?" Grandma Ava's face spoke to me from the projection springing out of my watch. "You done forgot about your poor old Grandma Ava? You didn't even call today."

"No, ma'am." I dropped my gaze. "I haven't forgotten about you. Today was really busy in here. And . . . it's my parents." I eyed the door and dropped my voice to a whisper. "They've been acting really weird."

"Well, of course they have. Anybody can see that."

I sat straight up. "Wait, really?"

"Shoot, yeah. All that money and fame, probably," she said. "Got them acting totally different. I ain't raise Stacy to be like that. But don't worry. I'll come to get you myself if I need to. Your parents think sending this little revbot to stay with me and cook for me is a fair exchange for not seeing my grandbaby, but they've got another thing coming."

"Oh," I sighed. "Yeah . . ." I swallowed the urge to tell her what was happening.

But I was worried. She didn't know about Futureland, or even my parents. We had all been gone from Atlanta for such a long time.

"Anyway, how are things going at school?" Grandma Ava's voice snapped me out of my thoughts.

"Well . . . wait—"

Grandma Ava's image blurred, and the faces of my crew—Angel, Earl, Rich, and Yusuf—emerged and swirled around. An incoming call. I had given them all prototype Futurewatches when we started the investigation as a team.

"Hey, Grandma, I'm getting a call. Can I call you back?"

"A call? At this time of night? Who do you think you are, young man? Everybody too busy for this old lady, huh? Just y'all wait. I'm gonna go to Biloxi to the casino and meet a nice older gentleman and—"

Click.

"What's up, y'all?" I asked.

Their faces came into focus.

No one spoke.

"Hello? Can y'all hear me? What's up? What's wrong? Y'all look like y'all have seen a ghost."

"He doesn't know," Angel murmured.

"Know what?" I asked.

"He has to know," Rich said.

"How could he not know?" Earl asked.

"Know what?" I shouted.

Nobody spoke. For a moment. And then, Yusuf.

"CJ . . . there's another kid missing."

MISSING

MICHELLE (JUJU) JULIEN

Height: 5'2" Weight: 115 lbs. Hair/eyes: Brown
Birthmark: Forehead

Juju is a 12-year-old Black American girl who was last
seen near Centennial Park, wearing blue jeans, a green
T-shirt, and a red woven bracelet on her left wrist.

CALL: (987) 555-0100

16

NOT SO FAST

Sunday, September 20, 2048
10:30 a.m.

B e there in thirty." I tapped my watch and sent the message to Yusuf.

No more doubting myself. No more letting paranoia trick me out of my intuition.

After the announcement and a second kid going missing, there was too much evidence to ignore. My bulletin board hologram filled up fast.

1. Southmore hacking Futureland Tech.
2. Missing kids.
3. ADRC trying to capture revs for . . . something?
4. Southmore swapping my real parents with revs (?)

Okay, okay. I wasn't quite sure about the last one yet. But things were starting to add up. Like Southmore getting "invited" to help run Futureland. My real parents would never do that. But if Southmore could somehow exchange them for fake versions of my parents who would do what he wanted them to do . . . Gah, I know. But I'm onto something.

I needed my friends to pull everything together. Angel and Earl had more research to share, and Rich said he'd ordered some cool spy tech online. We'd meet at Yusuf's house this time. At least, that was the plan.

I grabbed an apple from the fridge and went to leave in the elevator.

"Hold on," chef-rev Alejandro said. "What is the hurry?"

"I've got . . . I've got a study group," I lied. Yusuf lived close to Grandma Ava. If my pretend parents thought I was studying, it might buy me enough time away from Futureland to meet up with the crew and stop to see Grandma Ava for a bit after.

"Your parents have a special message for you. Your studies will have to wait. They would like you to meet them in the lab."

My heart froze. *Why?*

I nodded and Chef Alejandro went back to his cooking.

I slowly made my way to the lab, climbed down the entry hatch. My body tensed as I remembered my last time there—in the dark, scrambling around for evidence, tying up Woody.

I looked for him as I eased inside. But I turned to see Woody standing stiff and upright in a corner, eyes dim.

Someone had powered him down.

My pretend parents stood straight ahead. Their steps were rigid, jerky, like it hurt them to walk. But they smiled anyway.

"Good morning, Little Man," they said at the same time.

"Um, hi." I shuffled from foot to foot. My skin crawled at the sound of their voices.

"We'll get straight to the point," Dad said. "We have a task that we'd like you to complete. It shouldn't take long, but we realize we haven't been letting you help as much in the park. We're sorry. But now . . . we've found the perfect thing for your kid brain to help with."

I played their game. "Oh. Okay. Sure. What can I help with?"

"But first," Mom cut in, "we have a question. Have you been tampering with the security settings in Futureland? Specifically in Sports Summit and Wonder Worlds?"

My ears got hot. My heart started to race. "No."

"Don't lie to us, Cameron." Dad's voice dropped to a rasp.

"I—I wasn't tampering," I stuttered. "I was just . . . I was just making sure everything was safe. For the visitors."

"We understand your concern, Cam-Cam, but everything is going to be fine. This is *our* park."

Their park? My parents *always* talked about how Futureland was mine to take over one day. How it was all of ours, as a family.

"We know what's best," Mom continued. "It wasn't very responsible of you to mess around with security settings, and then to lie about it. Good thing a few of the Watchers noticed you in the exhibits after hours."

"You have Watchers . . . watching me?" I scanned the entire room, glancing at all the powered-down revs. My palms had started to sweat.

"Watchers watch everyone and everything in the park, Cam. It's for the safety of us all," Dad barked.

I flinched.

Silence stretched between us. I was just sure they could hear my heart pounding.

"Enough of this. Jeremy, tell him about the task." Mom crossed her arms and tapped her fingers.

"Certainly," Dad replied. "It's simple. Please go to the Mines of Tomorrow destiny and make sure the lights are working."

"Huh?" I said.

"*Please* go to the Mines of Tomorrow destiny and make sure the lights are working," Dad repeated, rasping.

"That's it? The lights?" I asked.

"Yes. We plan to extend operating hours, and we estimate more visitors will come to this destiny . . . and considering your point about safety, we just want to make sure the mines have enough light for everyone to navigate." Dad smiled.

A pained one.

"Okay. I'll call Dooley and head over to the Mines of Tomorrow right now."

"Dooley won't be available to accompany you," Mom said. "We have her busy with some other, very important matters."

My mouth felt like a desert. "You want me to go to the mines . . . alone?"

My pretend parents smiled, identical, their hands

neatly clasped at their waists. "Yes," they replied in unison.

My legs trembled as the Jet-Blur pod lowered me down at the center of the Mines of Tomorrow. Honestly, the mines had always given me the creeps. And I had never gone by myself. I was hoping it wouldn't be so bad—go in, check a few light switches, and be done.

Right? I crossed my fingers.

The Mines of Tomorrow was mainly a desert area—a dusty reddish-brown landscape with a few cacti sprouting here and there. Dozens and dozens of mounds of all sizes populated the area. Each mound had an opening—a tunnel, connected to the other mounds, making up a super-complex underground maze that Dad and Uncle Trey had designed. You could enter anywhere and find yourself on the complete opposite side of the Mines of Tomorrow by the time you escaped, with a chance to discover prizes, tokens, and rare souvenirs as you tunneled.

I wasn't feeling very adventurous. Like, at all.

I got out of the Jet-Blur pod and breathed in

the dry air. I set the wait timer on the pod to one hour so that I wouldn't have to call a new pod when I finished. I zipped up my special Mines of Tomorrow jumpsuit—a rugged one-piece designed to keep guests cool outside the mines and warm within. I tightened my hard hat and started to walk toward the nearest mound opening but froze in my tracks when I saw another person.

A rev? It was definitely someone, skittering at the sight of me and dashing into the mine entrance.

"Hey! Wait up! What are you doing here? Where are you going?" I jogged toward the mound opening.

And then wind hit me from behind.

"No!" I said as my Jet-Blur pod lifted into the air and zipped off.

I dropped to my knees and pounded the dust. I just knew I set that timer. How did this happen?

I checked my watch, thinking I could send an alert to Dooley or Mom or Dad to send another pod while I was in the mines, but the charge was fading fast. And it needed either sunlight or moonlight to replenish. It would be next to useless in the caves.

I decided to conserve my watch's energy. I tinkered with it for a second, trying to initiate Low-Power Mode to extend the charge, when I heard the echoes of cackles coming from inside the caves.

The hair on the back of my neck went straight. I stood, tapped my hard hat twice until the headlamp came on, and made my way into the mines.

I kept my hand along the wall as I walked deeper into the tunnel. Uncle Trey had taught me before to walk in straight lines for as long as possible in the mines. I wished he was with me. Whenever my parents got too far in their own world, I could always count on him to bring our family back down to earth. I didn't believe that vacation excuse one bit. And I was starting to worry that something bad had happened to him.

With my Futurewatch in Low-Power Mode, I'd need to navigate my own way out—the location feature would take too much juice, and I might not be able to get a pod back. I could see just fine for the first few minutes. Uncle Trey had installed motion-detecting lights in the walls every few yards in the tunnel.

But after a while, they stopped detecting. I found myself in total darkness.

I moved closer to the wall to inspect the lights that didn't operate. I focused my headlamp on them to try to determine the problem.

Turns out, the problem was simple.

The bulbs were gone.

I stared at the wall, bewildered at how so many bulbs could be missing. The only answer was that someone had removed them. It was the only way.

And that's when I heard the cackling again. And the footsteps.

I turned just in time to see two feet kicking up dust, bending a corner in the tunnels, burrowing deeper and deeper into the mines. I had a choice. Continue walking along the wall and keep an eye on my way out of the mines or follow the mysterious mine runner?

I exhaled deeply and took off running after them. I had to know who it was.

Once they realized I was chasing them, they laughed even harder. Dipping and dodging, corner by corner, making it almost impossible to keep up. I caught glimpses of them as my headlamp bobbed up and down from jumping over rocks and scooting around pits in the mines. The deeper we traveled, the darker it got, and more voices and laughs seeped through the walls, surrounding me.

I was out of breath and paused, noticing that my mysterious friend had mostly been running us in circles.

Left bend, right bend, around and around the

mines with no real direction. I couldn't keep chasing them forever. The next time they turned left, I went right and tapped my headlamp to kill the light. I gave my last burst of energy to push through the dark.

I heard the echo of their laugh growing closer and closer, until their outline came into view, running, laughing, looking backward over their shoulder.

Looking for me.

I dived into them and tackled them to the ground as we met in the middle of a clearing, deep at the center of the mines. We rolled around a couple times as they tried to escape my grip, but I pinned them down and sat on their stomach.

I tapped my headlamp twice and pointed it down at them, and for the first time, got a good look at my challenger.

It was a rev. The red rings around their eyes glowed fiercely under the light of my headlamp. They kept squirming, trying to free themselves of my weight, but they were too small, designed to appear only seven years old, maybe eight. Long, fluffy hair sprang from underneath their hard hat in every direction. Their almond skin matched the color of the mine dust, and they had a long scar on their right cheek. In between wriggling under me and grunting in frustration, the rev laughed and repeated the same phrase over and over again:

"Not . . . so . . . fast."

"Just be still!" I yelled, trying to pin down their shoulders with my hands. "I'm Cam Walker. My parents run this place."

"Cam Walker . . . not so fast," the rev shrieked, giggling with an evil glee and still trying to break away from me.

I reached behind the rev's neck and felt for their power-down button. Their eyes glowed again and their cheerful expression turned into a snarl. When they spoke again, their voice was like a growl.

"Not so fast," they barked, biting at my hand.

I pulled it back just in time.

A-a-activate safe mode!
You cause trouble, Cameron Walker.
Many ways to be lost. Many, many tunnels.
No commands here, Cameron Walker. These are *our* mines.
We can cause trouble, too. We can make you lost . . . and never found.
Are you going to hurt me?

17

#MISSINGKIDSMARCH

Monday, September 21, 2048
12:15 p.m.

The next day at school, I hurried to the lunch table before Rich, Angel, or even Earl. I needed to get it together. My hands trembled as I set my tray down and took my seat. I hadn't been able to get rid of the shaking since last night. Even when I locked myself in my room for the whole night. I barely slept. Every noise made me jump.

I put my head down, trying to breathe. I knew Angel or Yusuf would be here any minute. Friendship rule #1 was that I wasn't supposed to be on my own at school. They were taking their roles as my personal security guides very seriously.

I wasn't safe in Futureland. I wasn't safe at Grandma Ava's—not with Aurielle around. And now I wasn't even safe at school, with everyone asking me for park tickets.

"Hey, rich kid," a voice called out.

I looked up and gulped. A bigger kid stared down at me. Maybe a seventh or eighth grader. "You too good to respond?"

"No, it's not that," I replied. Sweat drenched my back.

"Running all over school with your little bodyguards, ignoring everyone. Word is that you won't give nobody any tickets to your fancy park. You could pay for the whole school to go, couldn't you?"

"It doesn't really work like that." My heart squeezed. "I'm sorry—I—"

"If you won't help me, then I'll help myself"—he grabbed my collar—"to some Future Passes. You better bring me two of them tomorrow. And every day you don't, I—"

The boy went flying midsentence. Angel had rammed him halfway across the lunchroom. Laughter erupted all around. The boy stomped out through the double doors.

Yusuf, Earl, and Rich ran up to the table, grinning.

"Is Angel gonna get in trouble for this?" I asked, both grateful that she did that for me and also worried.

"Hmm. Nah," Yusuf said. "That kid is always

bullying people. Teachers are probably laughing about it in secret."

Angel strode back to the table, brushing off her hands. "All in a day's work."

"Speaking of work, we've got a plan," Earl said. "Did Angel tell you?"

"What plan?" I asked.

"I can break it down." Earl pulled a binder of documents out of his backpack and passed it to me. Rich and Yusuf huddled around. Some of the papers were writings; some were drawings; others explained the writings and drawings. "Angel and I have been working hard on this. It's finally ready." Earl pointed at the pages. "If you're right—about the hacking, ADRC, and the pretend parents and missing kids—then this is going to help show everyone the truth." Earl smiled, proud of his work.

"This is amazing," I said. "You think it can work?"

"I believe in it," Angel said. "This could be a really good way to get them to slip up. Reveal themselves. If we even get so much as a hint of who it might be . . . you can break this whole case open."

"Cool," Rich said. "Only one problem. What do we do in the meantime? What happened to CJ in the mines was like some kinda freaky horror movie scene, bruh."

"Rich is right. CJ isn't safe in Futureland," Yusuf said. "What if you go stay with your grandma Ava?"

"Can't," I said. "I think that maybe Aurielle was sent there to spy on her. Playing like she's just cooking and cleaning up."

"Have you told your grandma?" Earl asked.

"I don't want to scare her. If she knows too much . . . she might be in even more danger."

"We can take shifts at your condo," Yusuf added. "Stay up nights? Somebody can come 'study' at the ship every night until we get a handle on this. Especially if your pretend parents are keeping Dooley away."

The mention of Dooley made my heart sink. I was losing my parents and my best friend a little each day.

"I appreciate it, guys, but we won't figure this out if I'm not in Futureland. It may not be a safe place for y'all. But I feel like I need to be there."

"What do you mean?" Earl asked.

"Well, my pretend parents had to know that there were no light bulbs in the mines," I said. "So they sent me there knowing those revs would catch me. But not hurt me. Only threaten me. Whoever is doing this . . . if they wanted to hurt me—"

"They could have already done it," Rich finished my sentence.

"Exactly. They want me in Futureland. They want me inside the park, keeping quiet."

"But why?" Yusuf asked.

"Well, I was thinking about that." I leaned forward to make sure no one heard me. "Whoever did this probably thinks that if I got hurt or went missing, my *real* parents' next step would be to care for me. Mom and Dad would close Futureland down until they were sure I was okay."

"So whoever it is must need Futureland to stay open to finish their plan," Earl said.

"Exactly."

"But who *needs* Futureland to stay open that bad?" Rich drummed his fingers on the table.

"Hopefully we find out," I said, passing the binder back to Earl.

After school, a crowd grew larger and larger outside of Eastside Middle School. Hundreds of people there, maybe even a thousand. I stood shoulder to shoulder with Angel, Earl, Yusuf, and Rich.

The search party for Iman and Juju was underway. All the parents who volunteered to help waited with signs and megaphones. Whispers crackled around us like popcorn. People talking about exposing the ADRC and bringing the missing kids home. Not wanting history to repeat itself like the 1980s in Atlanta.

One of the parents spoke into the megaphone: "For too long, this city has been attacked by gentrification. Our families who worked here for decades, making this city what it is, are being pushed out of it. We are losing our community, our history, and our safety. We have to fight back!"

The parent handed the megaphone to Angel. She started reading from a speech she had written. "There is something evil going on in Atlanta. Kids are disappearing. And we believe ADRC knows more than they are telling us. You all have seen our community centers turn into fancy loft apartments. You've seen business buildings plopped in the middle of parks and homes bulldozed for shopping centers. At the end of this rally, half of us will join the search committee to help Ms. Sheffield and Mr. Julien—the other half will march with us to ADRC headquarters and demand answers!"

The crowd cheered, powered up. I looked at Iman Sheffield's mom and Juju Julien's dad. They dabbed their eyes with tissues.

"What about Futureland?" someone yelled. "That's where those kids were."

"Everything was fine before that flying park came here!" came another voice.

I froze. Gulp.

I felt Angel flinch beside me. Yusuf put a hand on my shoulder.

More and more complaints about the park buzzed around me. I wanted to disappear.

Ms. Sheffield took the megaphone and stepped on the platform. "I'm pleading with you to calm down and listen. My child is lost. They've been lost for sixteen days. I've been in contact with the park, and they're investigating. You all came here because you said you wanted to help. You wanted to help bring our babies home."

Words bubbled up inside me. I couldn't let them think this about my *real* parents' greatest dream. I had to protect Futureland.

I put my hand in the air.

A hush fell over the crowd.

"Yes, young man?" Ms. Sheffield said.

"I—I have something to say." I tried to pull all the courage I had out of me. She waved me forward. I stepped up on the platform and looked out at the crowd. She handed me the microphone. It felt slippery in my sweaty hands. "I'm Cameron J. Walker. My parents built Futureland."

Whispers crackled through the crowd.

I cleared my throat. "I go to Eastside Middle School now. . . ."

Inhale, exhale. Here goes nothing.

"I know I'm just the Futureland kid to some of you. Honestly, I used to think that's the only thing I would ever be. But being in Atlanta, around friends, around people who care . . . has shown me that I can be more. That I *am* more. And I know my parents would be here if they could. This is their home, too. We will help find Iman and Juju. I promise."

The crowd was quiet. I looked out over all the faces. Different races, different backgrounds, all standing together, united. Out of the quiet, one voice sounded out. One voice with just one word.

"*March!*"

Soon, the phrase rose like a tidal wave across the whole crowd, hundreds of people shouting and pumping their fists, turning toward the ADRC building in the distance and preparing to go surround it.

"*March! March! March! March!*"

I smiled and turned to the crew. We grabbed our

bags and got ready to join the crowd on the way down-town.

Sirens screamed.

Dozens of police cruisers sped down the street. They drove onto the school lawn. Officers poured out of every car, running and shouting at the crowd.

"This is your only warning. You have two minutes to disperse. This is private property, and this gathering was not approved and cleared by the city or the sheriff's department. If you refuse to evacuate the premises, we will not hesitate to use force," one of the cops shouted.

"You can't do this!" one of the parents yelled.

My stomach dropped.

"Leave us alone!" Angel screamed. "We're going to find Iman Sheffield and Juju Julien! We're going to find their kidnapper, since you haven't."

The officer scoffed. "Don't you watch the news?"

"Huh?" I said.

"We already found the kidnapper. He's in custody."

THE ATLANTA DIARY DECLARATION

Atlanta's Premier Daily News Source

FUTURELAND EMPLOYEE ARRESTED ON SUSPICION OF KIDNAPPING

September 22, 2048

Alfred Abrams III, known to most as "Trey," was arrested Friday afternoon on suspicion of involvement with a string of local child disappearances in the Atlanta area. Abrams became a person of interest after the disappearance of Iman Sheffield, a 13-year-old from East Atlanta, on September 5.

For weeks, Abrams's whereabouts were unknown, but he was found Friday, outside the gates surrounding the floating theme park, trying to find his way back in, seemingly dazed and confused. When approached by an officer and questioned to determine whether he was trespassing, Abrams became combative and eventually resisted

CONTINUED ON NEXT PAGE

arrest. He was found in possession of a soccer jersey described as the one Iman Sheffield was last seen wearing, and a red woven bracelet police believe may belong to Michelle "Juju" Julien, another missing child.

Abrams has worked as an employee of Futureland for a number of years, mostly managing maintenance and repairs for the park's exhibits.

He was born and raised in Atlanta and has no history of prior arrest. When park directors Stacy and J. B. Walker were invited to comment on Abrams's arrest, they noted that they had not seen "Trey" in weeks, and that they could not provide any alibis for his activities. They expressed disappointment that he could be involved in something like this.

ASHLEY GRAHAM

Culture Correspondent & Digital Producer

Atlanta Mayor and CEO Team Up to Fix Futureland Problem

September 23, 2048

BY: THAÏS CADIEUX

The World Times. A blog of United States news, government, and politics for a global audience.

Bonjour. Bonsoir, world.

Mayor Ta'keya Raddish-Topston and Blaise Southmore, the CEO of the Atlanta Disuse and Redevelopment Corporation (ADRC), held a press conference yesterday to announce some big things.

Following the arrest of Trey Abrams on suspicion of kidnapping two kids that went missing after visiting Futureland, Mayor Topston and Mr. Southmore unveiled a new initiative to increase safety and security at the park until the case is resolved. Abrams is a Futureland maintenance worker and brother of park director Dr. Stacy Walker.

"We understand this is a big attraction," Mayor Topston said. "But safety is priority for the children of Atlanta. If our investigation finds that this park is unsafe, I have no problem authorizing Mr. Southmore and ADRC to take Futureland under their control and do whatever they need to do with it, for the good of the people."

Will Futureland become a thing of the past?

We'll see. The world is watching. Adieu.

18

DISPOSE

I stood frozen in front of Rich's TV. Every news station played the video of Uncle Trey struggling against the officer, fighting to get into Centennial Olympic Park and back to Futureland, and being handcuffed and stuffed into the squad car.

Tears streamed down my face. But I couldn't stop watching.

My head was a mess. I just couldn't make sense of it. All the evidence we'd collected made sense. But this . . . this came from left field.

Why would Uncle Trey kidnap Iman and Juju? And where in the world could he have been hiding all this time? Why would he show up now, of all times?

The news showed the swarms of people outside the park. Reports, angry parents, and more.

"When was the last time you saw your uncle?" Angel asked me.

"Been weeks. Which is weird." I shrugged.

"Are there any other suspects? Evidence? Anything that points away from him?" Yusuf asked.

"No," I said, defeat piling up in me. "That's why I have to figure this thing out. If I can prove that somebody is framing him, and we can get to the bottom of this ADRC thing, then maybe I can clear his name."

Yusuf turned the channel. Another breaking news report. A press conference with the mayor of Atlanta. "If Futureland is found to be unsafe, then I'll be giving control of the park to ADRC."

My heart seized.

"What does that even mean?" Angel leaned forward.

"My dad told me that if the ADRC says something is in 'disuse,' they get permission to take ownership of it," Earl said. "Then they can break it down and make whatever out of it. And the government gives them money to do all of this. That's how they can afford to build so many fancy things around the city."

I paced. Panic shot through me.

Everyone started to talk at once. I plugged my ears. Think. *Think.*

What do they want? The question tumbled over and over again in my head.

Then it hit me. "Wait!" I put my hand up. Everyone went quiet. "If Southmore and ADRC could take down Futureland and steal all its tech at once, then that's just two birds with one stone."

"So *that* was the motivation," Angel said.

"It has to be. For the hacking, for the missing kids, and probably for framing my Uncle Trey. And swapping out my parents with revs would only make the process easier," I said. "Southmore is the *only* person that needs Futureland open, needs me not to get hurt or go missing. If the park stays open and he's in control of security . . ."

"He could make anything go wrong. Then, when the city gives him control of Futureland, he can do whatever he wants with it," Yusuf added.

"Yep."

"Wow, that's really evil," Rich said.

"The evilest," Angel said.

"I kept thinking and thinking and thinking—what would someone do with Futureland? I mean, it's the most complex park in the world. It would take years to learn how to run. You guys told me that ADRC could turn a historic home into a coffee shop. *So,* I thought, *what would a company turn Futureland into?* That's when I started thinking . . . maybe it's not the big park that they want. Maybe it's something smaller. And Futureland has smaller things that are valuable. Hundreds and hundreds of them."

"The revs?" Yusuf said.

"The revs," we all said in unison.

"Bet they want to steal them," Earl said.

"Probably want to sell them or have them in your houses." Rich started rattling off all the ways a rev could be used. "ADRC could charge a fortune for that sort of thing. My dad would probably send my mom one."

Rage bubbled up in me. "Southmore is going to try to steal everything."

"The missing kids . . . they're just a distraction." Earl shook his head, mad.

"To turn people against the park and your parents, so that when the city finally gives up on Futureland, nobody will stick up for them," Angel said.

"He'll be all like, 'Futureland just ain't safe. Look at all the kids going missing. I'll make everything better,'" I said in my best Southmore voice.

All my friends laughed. "Wow, Cam, you do a really good Southmore impression," said Angel.

"Yeah, you sound just like him," Rich agreed. "But how can we know for sure your intuition is right?"

I grabbed my Future-vision goggles from my bag.

"There's one person who would know for sure. I have to find her."

Dooley.

As I hit the last stretch of road toward Eastside Middle School, I spotted Dooley standing at the corner.

My heart jumped. Even though she hadn't been acting like *my* Dooley for weeks, she was still my best friend and only hope.

Walker Way of Living #9—Stick together, no matter what.

But it was getting harder and harder.

Talking to her had to work. I took a deep breath. "Hey, D," I said. "Remember that time you said you weren't a rev anymore? What did you mean?"

"I'm sorry, Cameron. I have no recollection of that event." She gazed forward.

"Be cool, D. You're telling me you don't remember anything about when we had that conversation?"

"I wish I could, Cam, but I can't. I'm sorry."

My stomach twisted. My plan felt like a failure. I thought if I could get her to tell me about that day, then I could find out who taught her those questions or changed her.

"You're walking much slower than usual, Cameron," she said. "Are you not feeling well? Is this why you wanted me to walk you to school this morning?"

I shrugged. "No, D." I needed her.

When we finally got to the school, I paused, and I turned to face Dooley. "See you later," I said.

"Galactic Gator," she whispered back.

Just like before.

But this day would be different.

An alert pinged on my Futurewatch. My friends and I had synchronized our Futurewatches. It was 7:48 a.m. sharp, two minutes before the class warning bell. Yusuf should be on his way into the office to strike up a conversation with Mrs. Parker. She was a huge basketball fan and thought Yusuf was "the cutest thing."

After two minutes of small talk, the class bell would ring, and Mrs. Parker would get to work herding students to class, especially a group of annoying loud kids stationed right outside her office. Earl had offered them extra pizza at lunch for a week to give her a hard time and take forever to follow her rules.

My watched pinged again: 7:50. I scooted around the back of the school, pulled out my Future-vision goggles, and tapped on my Futurewatch. "Rich, you there?"

I overheard him.

Cough, cough. "No thanks, Pierre. No more tea. Yeah,

I'm still sick." *Cough, cough.* "Thanks, Pierre." I heard a door open and close as Pierre left the room. "My bad, CJ. Yeah, I'm here. You ready?"

Rich had faked sick to stay home and be the command center today.

"Yep," I said while pulling one of his mini-drones out of my backpack.

"Okay, okay. You got it set up?"

"Doing it now." I set it on the ground.

"It's ready. I can see it in the app."

It started to hover, then cruised left, then right, then soared higher into the sky, Rich controlling it all the way from his house.

I turned in the direction Dooley left. I was going to follow Dooley. The Future-vision goggles would allow me to stay far enough behind her. And Rich's drone? Well, Rich's drone was going to follow me and get footage.

"Here I go," I said. "By the way, your cough sounds really fake."

"This fake cough got me the day off, Cameron Jethro Walker," Rich replied. "And it got you a command officer. Now, get to moving."

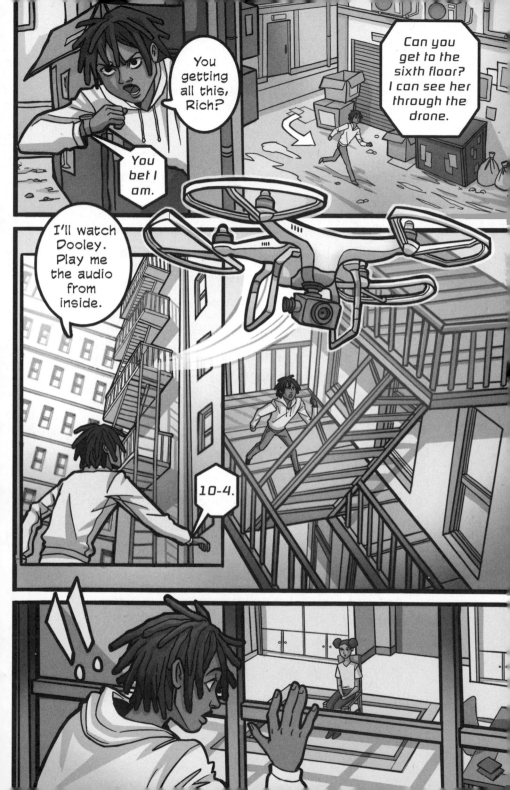

Dooley sat in the middle of the room in a single chair, hands folded in her lap, staring straight ahead. Her orange irises glowed. She didn't move.

I gasped.

She was transferring information. But to where? What information?

I tugged on the window and it cracked. I froze, scared. I'd been caught. I was sure of it. I waited for someone to come running out.

But nothing happened.

Dooley's eyes still swirled neon. I squeezed through the window. The hair on my neck stood up. A pit burned in my stomach.

Tapping footsteps echoed.

Blaise Southmore entered the warehouse room. He stood over Dooley, then pulled up a chair and sat across from her. He fidgeted with his phone before setting it on his lap.

"Are you seeing what I'm seeing?" I whispered to Rich.

"You bet I am. He's recording on his phone, too."

"Can you play the drone audio through the earpiece?" I asked.

"Gimme a sec."

Dooley's eyes darkened. She blinked, then looked at Southmore and cringed.

He leaned back in his chair and crossed his legs. "You know what time it is, darling," he said. "Voice recognition. Southmore. Analysis Mode."

Dooley winced, her body convulsing. "Code word required." She grimaced.

"Martha," Blaise said.

He'd coded her to follow commands from a specific voice. Just like me.

Dooley's face went blank and she went into Response Mode, just like the rcvs when Uncle Trey had to do repairs on them. Like the time I *tried* to make Dooley go into Response Mode, when she came to Rich's house and told us to stop investigating.

"Do you have the latest surveillance footage of Cameron Walker?" he asked.

"The latest information has been uploaded," Dooley replied.

"Good. Ask him more questions. We need to keep an eye on him and his little friends."

Dooley rattled off everyone's first and last names and where they lived. My heart thundered.

"Yes. Will do," she replied.

"We need to find a way to leak something from

Futureland that adds to the police's case against Trey. Good thinking on framing the kid's uncle. I was getting tired of keeping him locked up in here anyway. But we need more evidence to make it stick."

Dooley didn't speak. I thought I would vomit.

"Have you updated the security protocols in the park like I asked?" Southmore said.

"The park security restrictions have been scaled back. In-park surveillance has been shut down."

"Good. The Walker kid sneaking into the lab cost us that first time. Too much suspicion to go through with plan A, but we have more control now that I've reprogrammed the revs. There's no telling what sort of trouble they'll cause." A sick smile spread across his face. "I need everything that can possibly go wrong in Futureland to go wrong."

The realization that I was right settled over me. He'd ruin Futureland's reputation and steal the technology.

"Maybe a kid will fall and get hurt or get tossed by a rev—make my job easy," Southmore continued. "Have you finished uploading the top-secret data and instructions for the Futureland tech?"

Dooley didn't speak.

"Um, hello? You hear me speaking, now don't you? Do you have the data or not?"

"Many of the classified data files and instructions for usage are . . . heavily protected, large files. I have started to upload some. I estimate it will take longer than expected to fully transfer everything."

"Well, I estimate you better make it happen as soon as possible." Southmore snarled at her. "Without that data, none of this means anything. It's time for my very own Future City."

"Future City: an exclusive, on-the-ground, living development incorporating Futureland technology into the real world. By demolishing low-income neighborhoods west and south of Atlanta, ADRC can make space to construct the most technologically advanced city in the world and populate it with the wealthiest people. Future City will be the first of its kind in the United States, with many others to follow," Dooley rattled off.

"Yes, yes, I know what it is," Southmore snapped. "It's *my* plan, after all. I even talked to the Walkers about it when I visited Futureland's first opening fifteen years ago. I was just another face in the crowd then. When I met them a few weeks ago, they didn't even remember me." He smirked.

My mouth dropped and hung open.

"Now, back to the kid. What's the plan for him?"

Southmore asked. "I need you to dispose of him, his friends, too, and all the other kids. All of them need to go."

Dooley's eyes spun. "Comprehension error."

"The kids. I can't risk having them pop up. They need to be missing *permanently*. It's your job to make that happen. Understand?"

Dooley didn't speak.

"Ugh. Goodness gracious. Archive command, dispose of all targets."

"Command . . . archived," she droned.

"Finally. Resume Standard Mode," Southmore said.

The light dimmed around Dooley's eyes, but I heard her sniffles through my Future-vision goggles.

"Get back to work." Southmore stood. "And stop with that crying, before I delete your emotion code. By the way—does Cameron suspect anything about his parents?"

Dooley was quiet for a moment. "He knows."

"Well, keep him quiet. Those rev stand-ins are working quite nicely. With his parents gone, no one will ever be able to tell." He rubbed his chin. "Wish we could just go ahead and replace that kid of theirs. The software isn't good enough to send a rev to school. We just need a little while longer, and then we can frame his parents, too."

A door opened. I heard the *click-clack* of high heels. I craned to look.

It was the rev I had met in Bright Futures with the missing brother. She smiled at Southmore, the corners of her mouth twitching. Her irises spun bright red, instead of orange.

He's hacked her, too, I thought.

"Come, Master Southmore. I've prepared your plan for this evening," she said in a deep, raspy voice.

Their footsteps echoed into the hallway. Dooley stood up and looked around the warehouse. Her eyes looked in my direction, and she froze for a moment.

I crouched deeper into the shadows and watched her exit the building.

"You got all that?" I asked Rich.

"Every word. I turned the recording feature on, too. We got ourselves some evidence. Bringing the drone around now. Let's get out of this place. It gives me the creeps."

"You can say that again," I said.

I climbed out the window and down the fire escape. Rich's drone landed near me, and I stuffed it down into my pack, along with my Future-vision goggles.

I jogged toward downtown, going over everything I had heard in my head.

Dispose of the kids.

Ruin Futureland forever.

Future City.

My real parents . . . gone.

We had to get this information to somebody quick. Somebody we could trust. But who?

I turned a corner and thought I saw someone—or something—in the corner of my eye. I whipped around and looked over my shoulder, but there was nothing there.

I kept jogging, slower now, more cautious. I rubbed my eyes. Maybe I needed to go to Rich's house.

Or maybe I was just paranoid.

The thing is, I could have sworn I saw someone. For only a second, a half second. I thought I saw a face peeking around the corner.

A face on a head with two afro-puffs.

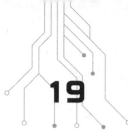

19

PURPOSE

Friday, September 25, 2048
3:00 p.m.

"The 1996 Olympic Games were a very big deal for Atlanta, and the city was extremely proud to play host to the athletes and guests," Mr. Chesterfield, my social studies teacher, said.

I barely listened. I couldn't stop thinking about Dooley. I scribbled in my notebook. It spilled over with everything I'd collected.

Southmore. Dooley. Future City. ADRC. Spy. Plan. Sabotage.

". . . very tragic event of bombings in the downtown area that hurt many people, and the perpetrator was unknown for quite some time . . ."

Missing kids. Where could they be? I thought hard. Dooley hadn't responded when Southmore asked her about the kids. Maybe there was still a chance that they could be found. But ADRC probably owned hundreds of buildings in Atlanta, like the warehouse where Southmore interrogated Dooley. The kids could be at any of them, and that was if we were lucky. There was no way the crew and I could possibly search them all.

I jammed my pencil into my notebook until the lead broke. I held it up, and Mr. Chesterfield motioned that I could go sharpen it.

"Eventually," said Mr. Chesterfield, still teaching, "the perpetrator was identified and tracked. The FBI pursued him, but he escaped into a national park in North Georgia—thousands of miles of forests—and evaded capture for years."

I froze at the pencil sharpener and turned slowly to look at the slides Mr. Chesterfield was showing on the screen. It was an overhead photo of treetops stretching mile after mile after mile, farther than the eye could hope to see.

"Mr. Chesterfield?" I raised my hand.

"Yes, Cameron?"

"So the guy who did the bombings hid in the national park and they couldn't find him . . . for years?"

"Yes, exactly. His survival training helped him navigate the wilderness. The park was simply too big for police to search. Too many places to hide."

Mr. Chesterfield turned back around to continue the lesson. My mind spun, red lights flashing, light bulbs lighting up . . . I remembered something that the leader of the mine-revs had said when I was there. *There are many tunnels here. Many, many ways to get lost . . . and never be found.* They were talking about the mines, but that same thing was true about all of Futureland! Anybody that knew their way around the park could find endless places to hide. And who knew their way around the park better than Dooley? Besides, it was the one place *nobody* would look for missing kids. It was just too easy.

I bolted from the pencil sharpener back to my desk and grabbed my pack. I turned on my heel and zipped right back out of the classroom, fumbling with my Futurewatch, trying to get a message out.

"Cameron? Cameron!" Mr. Chesterfield called.

I didn't stop.

Angel and Earl sat with me as we waited for Ms. Sheffield and Mr. Julien—Iman's and Juju's parents—to pull up at the park across from Eastside Middle. Yusuf had basketball practice, and Rich had already gone home. I'd call them later.

The parents hopped out of the car and walked fast toward us.

"Cam? Kids? Is everything all right? We came as soon as we could." Mr. Julien's face crinkled with worry.

"Yeah, yeah, no. Everything is fine. I think I have some information that could help us find Juju and Iman," I said.

Ms. Sheffield gasped and put her hand over her mouth.

"Um . . . okay," I started. "I think Iman and Juju are closer than we think. ADRC has been using surveillance to keep track of what's going on in Futureland, and Blaise Southmore has been changing a lot of settings in the park."

"Surveillance?" Mr. Julien said. "Why would that be necessary?"

"It's kinda tough to explain, but—"

"Changing settings? What does this have to do with Iman, Cam?" Ms. Sheffield asked.

I sighed. "Okay, okay. I have a hunch that Juju and Iman are . . . that they're still in the park. I think whoever took them is hiding them there. And always has been."

Both parents looked unsettled but didn't speak for a moment.

"But the police . . . they searched the park. . . ." Ms. Sheffield started to rock.

"Yes," I said. "But, with surveillance, ADRC could have known where they were searching and moved Iman and Juju before they were found. Futureland is huge. Way too big to search quickly."

"We don't know if Southmore is working with the police, either," Angel said, trying to help.

"Cameron," Mr. Julien said. "Every moment we spend not trying to find Juju . . . is another moment I have to spend wondering if we'll ever find her. They wouldn't let us into the park even if we wanted. And I just can't afford to waste time searching places that have already been searched. I'm sorry."

"But—" I started.

"Cameron, sweetie." Ms. Sheffield patted my hand. "I have to agree. And I have a safety committee meeting in about twenty minutes. I appreciate you thinking so hard about this. I really do. If you come up with any other ideas, let me know, okay?"

"But, wait! Please!" I pleaded, but they headed back to the car.

As they left, Grandma Ava pulled up in her old town car and honked the horn.

"See you later, Angel." I left the bench and hopped into Grandma Ava's car, and we started driving home.

"Grandma." I stared out of the window as we rode slowly down the street. "What do you do when everything is falling apart?"

"Hmm." She thought for a moment. "Trey once asked me the same question. You remind me so much of him sometimes. Well, baby, when everything is falling apart, you have to find the thing that can keep it all together." She was quiet for a moment. "For your parents, that thing was you. Their dream was always to build something that could take care of you for your entire life. That park became everything to them. That was their purpose. You were their purpose."

"What if my purpose is different from what everybody thinks it is?" I ask.

"There's no shame in that," she replied. "Your parents had a dream, and they made it happen. But that doesn't have to be your dream. Parents may say they want their kids to be this or that. Goodness, I wanted Stacy to be a dentist. Can you believe it?

"But what we *really* want, as parents, is for our babies to have enough freedom to find their own purpose. To live for themselves and make their dreams come true. If you have a dream, you have to follow it, Cam. That's why your parents worked so hard, baby. Not so you could run a park. But so you could follow your dream."

I kept staring out of the window as my heart felt like it might burst. No kid had ever done what I was trying to do. Especially no kid that looked like me, and in a city like Atlanta at that, going up against the evilest evil.

I wasn't giving up. No way. Detective Cam was here to stay. I had to do this. For Uncle Trey. For my real parents. For Dooley. For my family.

The dream is the truth.

Just like in Futureland.

It was time for me to dream big.

20

WONDER WORLDS

Friday, September 25, 2048
10:00 p.m.

I sat in Rich's car watching dozens and dozens of police guarding the gates outside Centennial Olympic
Park. I craned to look. Hundreds of them. There had
to be police inside the park area, too, below Futureland. And at this point, probably even police inside
Futureland.

To be fair, my parents had texted me during the day
to let me know that Futureland would have around-
the-clock police protection.

But I didn't imagine anything like this.

"Slow down, Pierre," Rich said as he let the mini-
drone fly from his palm into the night sky. He flew
the machine around the opposite side of the park

as we circled the block. "Yeah, CJ. It's looking ugly. Cops all over the entire park. Do you know what time they're leaving?"

"I think this is a twenty-four/seven thing," I said.

"Perhaps, if I may, Mr. Richardson . . . ," Pierre said.

"Yeah, sure. Got an idea, P?" Rich turned around

"Maybe you all could take advantage of a shift change."

"Hmm. What do you mean?" Rich asked.

"Well," Pierre continued. "If the security services are scheduled around the clock, they must be working in shifts. When one shift leaves, it may present an opportunity to sncak in undetected."

"Hmm. Great idea, Pierre," I said.

"So where are you thinking?" Rich asked as we darted behind trees and shops and anything else we could hide behind, making our way through the park.

"Well, the mines, for one," I said, shivering at the thought.

"The mines? Didn't you already go there?"

"Yeah, so it would probably be the last place Southmore would imagine I'd go back to."

"Good point."

"A few other places, too. The Obsidian Imaginarium isn't big enough yet. And places like Future Trek have too many visitors, too much traffic. Maybe in one of the closed destinies, like Wonder Worlds. Or maybe even—"

"Shhh," Rich said.

We crouched as two patrol officers walked by our hiding spot on the trail.

Great. Dangerous revs *and* cops in our way. Perfect.

We held our breath until they passed by. Sweat soaked both of our foreheads.

"Dang that was close." Rich panted. "Where to first?"

Don't do this, Cam. Please. Stay away.

A chill ran through my body. I heard the voice quietly, but clearly, like it was in the wind.

It was louder the second time. *Please, Cam. I don't want you to get hurt. Leave Futureland now.*

Dooley. Speaking directly into my head through my Future-vision goggles.

I couldn't let her throw me off.

"Let's try Wonder Worlds first," I said. "The mines are far, and they're really big. It'll be easier to start smaller."

Don't make me do this, Cam.

I shook my head to get her voice out. I wished she'd never updated my goggles.

"You all right?" Rich said.

"Yeah, come on," I said. "Let's just go."

Futureland was dark and quiet—as quiet as I'd ever seen it. The Millennium Marketplace was frozen in silence, the shops and eateries empty. The signs were dirty, and the trash cans overflowing. This hardly seemed like the same place it had been my whole life.

We found our way to the Wonder Worlds. The castle windows dark ahead. This exhibit had been open two seasons ago in Tokyo, but not since. Without Uncle Trey around to make the necessary repairs, I wasn't sure if it would ever be ready for park guests again. Perfect hiding place, if you ask me.

"This way." I led Rich down a side path and straight to the castle. The grounds twisted into four different mazes with tall walls of bushes, each one designed to be an adventure all on its own before a guest ever got to the castle. Dad had played with me here when I was little, showing me the fastest way through.

"There are so many doors," Rich said, looking up at the castle. It was covered in doors of all shapes and sizes with little mirrors that revealed different versions of yourself off on different adventures.

But instead of seeing reflections of me and Rich running across a life-size board game like Monopoly, or maybe inside our favorite video game, there was nothing.

"It'll take us forever," Rich complained.

I said, "Let's just run by every mirror and see if anything catches our eye."

"You go left on the ramp and I'll go right." Rich pointed.

Nerves shot through me.

You leave me no choice, Cam. Turn back now. This is your last chance.

Dooley's voice again. Even louder. Her voice filled up all the space in my head. I closed my eyes and plugged my ears.

Last chance, last chance, last chance . . .

Rich shook my arm. I almost fell. "Helloooo? You all right?"

"My bad. Let's go."

"Okay, I'm going this way." He dashed off to the right.

I went left, hustling up the ramp, stopping only for a second at each mirror to look inside. I saw all the regular stuff—me as a Pokémon trainer, me on a *Fortnite* mission, blah, blah. We could have spent hours behind each of those hundreds of doors searching for Iman and Juju. About halfway up the ramp, around door number seventy, I got frustrated.

What if this didn't work?

"Find anything yet?" Rich asked.

"Not yet!" I yelled back. "We're almost at the top. Then we can move on."

I passed a couple more mirrors, then froze. I saw a flicker of movement out the corner of my eye.

I could have sworn I saw a reflection in the mirror on the door behind me.

Except, well . . . the reflection wasn't mine.

I took steps back and looked into the oval mirror. I didn't see a spectacular world or a magical landscape. All I saw was her.

Dooley.

Hands at her sides and her head lowered. Through the mirror, she glared.

You left me no choice, Cam. I'm sorry.

"Dooley! No!" I snatched open the door.

Nothing.

No Dooley.

No world.

I closed the door and opened it again but saw the same.

Rich screamed.

My breath stopped short, and my heart beat faster.

I rushed around to his side of the ramp, fearing the worst. What if he had fallen off? From this height, I didn't want to think about what would happen if he hit the ground without a cushion. The safety measures of Wonder Worlds weren't active right now.

I spotted him struggling against the doorframe.

Two brown hands had him by the shirt. Rich leaned back, trying to get away. He struggled as they tightened their grip.

I ran and ran and ran until I finally got to his level. I rushed over to him and grabbed the back of his shirt, pulling him against the resistance of the force behind the door. "Hold on!"

All the arm strength I had drained out of me. I dug my heels in, then jerked Rich as hard as I could.

We tumbled backward. Rich bumped me over the ramp. I grabbed on to the ledge and swung hundreds of feet in the air.

"Help!" I yelled.

Rich leaned over and yanked me back up onto the ramp. We collapsed.

"You okay?" He panted.

"I think so. That was wild. Are you okay?" I asked.

"I think so. Yeah, what was that—" He screamed.

I turned to look. The Wonder Worlds door snapped open.

I froze.

Two hands yanked him by the waist. In a flash, I spotted Dooley.

The door slammed closed.

"Noooo!" I screamed, trying to yank it back open.

I'm sorry, Cam. We're almost out of time.

I balled up my fists and gritted my teeth.

No. I couldn't lose Rich. Not like this.

I couldn't let this be the end.

THE REALM OF REALITIES

I didn't enter one of the many virtual realities of Wonder Worlds when I passed through the door. Instead, I stood confused at the entrance of a place I had been many times before. But never like this.

The Realm of Realities.

So, wait. Let's back up.

A door in Wonder Worlds had led me not into a virtual reality designed for guests, but to the starting point inside a totally different park destiny?

That wasn't supposed to happen.

Maybe it was a glitch. Or a secret. Like, Dad could have designed it that way for quick travel between destinies. I had no idea. I thought I knew about all of Futureland's secret pathways and hidden areas, but this was a new one to me.

I'm not quite sure what Mom and Dad were thinking when they created the Realm of Realities. Maybe when they were young and outrageous (Mom always says I'm outrageous), they decided to create a topsy-turvy world with all kinds of wacky attractions. Maybe they had one too many lumi-pops before bed, dreamed wild things, and decided to bring them to life. Either way, there wasn't a lot that made sense in the RoR. It was kind of like a parking lot for Futureland's greatest exhibits that weren't that great. A sky-high space needle with a dangling ski-lift wrapped around it, like Saturn's rings. A building shaped like a cracked egg with a house of horrors inside the yolk. An underwater kingdom. Twisted trees. A mountain with roller-coaster chutes weaving and looping all around. You name it.

The Realm of Realities was Futureland's home for the absurd.

I walked around the destiny, unsure of where to go. It seemed livelier than usual, especially for an off day at the park. The trees with double trunks twisted together danced to the music playing across the destiny—a slow, distorted carnival theme. The ski lifts and roller-coaster cars whipped around their tracks without any passengers. Dooley had come through the same door as me with Rich in her clutches, but did she land here? Was she still here? Or did the portal put her somewhere else? I had told Rich that we'd need to be able to outsmart Dooley to figure this thing out, and here I was, failing. I had lost Rich, I might never find Iman and Juju, and pretty soon, the news would get out.

Yet another missing child.

Then I'd be a crazy kid who thought his parents were revs, with a robot best friend who was a kidnapper. Or worse—the kid whose uncle was accused of kidnapping Iman and Juju and who was the last one seen with Rich; an accomplice.

Futureland would be officially over. Our lives would be over.

I opened the door to the cracked-egg haunted house and shouted inside.

"Hellooooo?" My voice echoed back to me raspy and deep, a monster version of me.

I moved on and sat down on a giant sunflower in a field of dancing plants. My chest filled with panic. I was failing at everything. Futureland wasn't my place. I was no good at being a detective. And now, after I worked so hard and worried so much about making friends, I was leading them into danger. Danger I couldn't rescue them from.

I wished so badly that I could go back to the times before Atlanta. Before I lived on the ground, before this whole mess.

I missed when Dooley and I acted like best friends. . . .

When Mom and Dad would let us have secret picnics in the park on off days . . .

When the Walker Ways of Living still meant something . . .

I kept walking around the destiny, letting a multicolored sidewalk lead my path. Each square lit up a different hue of neon as I stepped on it. I took a step and noticed something etched into the concrete below.

Handprints. These were my handprints, and Mom's and Dad's, and even Dooley's. I remembered the day. We came here to play, and Dad said we could leave a personal stamp in the concrete, just like he and his friends used to do in Washington, DC, when he was a kid. Underneath all our names and handprints, there was something else drawn in the wobbly font of my finger.

#1 Always make time for each other.

Wait.

. . .

. . .

No way, that would be too simple.

I shut my eyes tight and thought back to our last secret picnic before we came to Atlanta. Dad had been telling us all summer that he was working on something special. Something we could all appreciate as a family.

We had packed our picnic baskets and took a Jet-Blur pod to the Realm of Realities. He walked us around all the wacky attractions to the rear of the destiny and into a small building shaped like an hourglass. He turned a dial, and we walked through the building and into a courtyard with Mom's favorite plants, butter-flies, and a big tree to picnic under.

We ate and laughed and played for what felt like forever. I thought we might be late getting a move on to Atlanta, but I was having so much fun with my family that I didn't want it to be over. So I didn't say any-thing. Eventually, though, Dad did say something.

"I'm sorry, Cam. We're almost out of time. We have to keep it moving."

When we left the Hourglass House and got back to our condo, I looked at our clock in the kitchen and noticed what seemed impossible.

Only one hour had passed. I ran around the apart-ment, checking all the clocks, but they all said the same thing. Mom and I were convinced we had spent most of the day at the picnic. Had it been an hour or eight? To Dad, the answer was simple.

"Both. This is my greatest creation yet. Time is suspended in here by a factor of eight." My dad had always loved Walker Way of Living #1. So much that he took it literally. When we didn't have enough time as a family, he *made* time. Created it. Out of thin air.

"We'll always be able to make Walker Way of Living number one count," he said, "even when we're short on time."

We're almost out of time.

That's what Dooley's voice had said to me right before she pulled Rich through the Wonder Worlds portal! She was sending me a message! I had to go and check the one place nobody would have ever dreamed of checking—

Because nobody knew about it. Nobody but us.

I ran back through the fields, bouncing myself off sunflower cushions and bounding over the hills of the destiny to the top. The Hourglass House was set far back in a wildflower field before the mountain range, but past all the attractions. I tapped my personal code into the keypad on the door and turned the mini-hourglass door handle, watching the sands begin to spill into the bottom chamber. The inside was just as I remembered it—like a countryside, or an orchard. The air smelled like hickory trees and sweet flowers. I spied a small cottage off in the distance—that was it.

I dashed up the hill as quickly as I could, rounded the cottage, and started toward the tree.

The closer I got . . . I thought I could make out . . . could it be?

The figures under the tree started to take shape and came into clearer view. I sprinted up to them and knelt.

They were all there. My breath got stuck in my chest. I couldn't believe it.

Mom, Dad. Iman, Juju, and Rich, swaying softly under the gigantic cherry blossom tree, in a daze. Someone had tied each of them by their wrists and ankles and even gagged their mouths with a cloth. I removed Rich's gag first and shook the dizziness out of him.

"Rich! Rich! Are you okay?"

"CJ! You left me? You let me get snatched?! How could you? Just wait until I—" I ignored Rich's big mouth and went to my parents.

"Mom? Dad?" I took their faces in my hands and rubbed them gently, my own tears forming. "It's me. It's Cam." My dad blinked several times and looked at me, confused, then at my mom. Mom looked confused at first, too, but then something clicked in her mind and her eyes got big.

"Cam. My baby. You came to save us," she said, exhausted.

I hugged her neck as she started to cry. I took their binds off, and then the three of us did the same for Iman, Juju, and Rich. Everyone stood up, stretched out, and tried to get their bearings.

"Where are we?" Juju asked, holding her head in both hands.

"We're inside Futureland, believe it or not," I said.

"How long have we been here?" asked Iman.

"We've been looking for you since the park opened. So . . ." I did some math in my head. "Twenty days, for you, Iman."

"Then it's the same for us," Dad said.

"What?" I gasped.

"We got snatched on opening night, too. At least, that's the last night I remember clearly." He thought hard. "Yes, we landed in Atlanta, had our big investors meeting—you know, the one where we usually let everybody down easy and tell them that Futureland will be okay without their money. But soon after that, they came after us. Whoever wanted us gone wasted no time."

"Weird. Why doesn't it feel that long?" Iman asked.

"Time moves differently in here," I explained. "And the settings on the chamber were reversed— I noticed when I came in. It's been reprogrammed, so instead of time moving eight times faster in here, it's moving eight times slower. So it should have only felt like—"

"Two and a half days," Mom said.

"We know who's doing this!" shouted Rich at my parents. "It's Blaise Southmore! And the fake versions of you. And Dooley!"

"We've seen Dooley," recalled Dad, rubbing his head. "She comes here. She brought us food and water. But everything is so cloudy in my memory."

"Fake versions of us?!" Mom's voice squeaked with concern.

"There's a lot to explain, Mom, but we don't have much time. Dooley is the one who snatched you and brought you here. But I finally know why. For right now, I need you to protect Rich and Iman and Juju. You have to keep them safe.

"Dad, I need to know how to reset the security codes for the park. I need to know how to make everything exactly how it was one hour before we landed twenty-six days ago—the rides, the revs, everything."

"Big Man, I can give you the codes, but are you sure? You don't want our help? This sounds dangerous," Dad said, his eyes full of worry.

"Trust me," I reassured him. "It's between me and a friend."

ME & A FRIEND

Saturday, September 26, 2048
Midnight

I raced toward our family condo as quickly as I could from the Realm of Realities. My parents kept the reset codes in a locked cabinet in our kitchen. Can you believe it? The most precious information in all of Futureland, sitting in a random cabinet next to some Future Flakes. Sometimes the correct answer is the simplest one.

I concentrated hard. My feet almost flew, from destiny to pathway, trail to platform.

"Dooley. I know you can hear me. I've figured it out. We can end this," I said into the mic on my Futurevision goggles.

I kept running.

"Dooley!"

Only silence.

And then . . . I heard her.

It's too late, Cam. He's coming for me. He's coming for all of us.

I ran even harder. When I got to the condo, I climbed up on the counter and fished out the codes, then zipped back out of the door toward the elevator.

The doors parted.

I froze.

Two policemen faced me.

"Hey, kid! What are you doing in here?"

Uh-oh.

I dipped around them and headed to the staircase. I needed to get to the center of the park. If I could activate the codes from there, the radius of the electrical signal would be wide enough to make sure everything was reset back to normal.

At least, that's what Dad *thought* would happen. He had never performed a full park reset before.

Walker Way of Living #3. Do the best you can.

I hopped into a Jet-Blur pod and took to the skies. All the police swarming the park would know I was here now, but at least they wouldn't be able to grab me. I crossed my fingers and hoped that I had enough time after landing to launch the reset.

I steered the pod to the middle of the park, landing

in the clearing right outside the entrance to the Obsidian Imaginarium. It landed with a thud, and I bounced up and down as it skidded across the ground.

The walls retracted, and I crawled out. Through the dust swirling in the air, I spotted Dooley's silhouette.

"How'd you know?" Dooley asked.

"Call it intuition," I said.

"I'm sorry, Cam. I—"

"You had no choice. I understand."

"He was going to hurt you. He had eyes on you everywhere. I was the first one he took. He reprogrammed me and scrambled up all of my code. He threatened to hurt your parents before commanding me to get rid of them. After he made copies of them, he didn't care what happened to your mom or dad, or you, or anybody. I had to do what he said." She hung her head. "I had to do what he said . . . to save *you*."

"And you did save me, Dooley. You saved all of us. We're still here, ready to fight back. We still have time!"

She looked up at me and shook her head slowly. "We're out of time. He's coming for me now, and he'll find you, too. If you reset the park, he'll destroy us all. He can't have anyone know what he's done. Your mom, dad, the kids . . . if they're still in here, they'll never leave. This entire park is swarming with his workers.

He's paid all the police. There's no hope for me, but you can still escape. You have to go now. Let me help you."

"And leave my parents and friends?! Dooley, no! There has to be another way."

"I have no more limits, Cam. You can only give a rev so much knowledge without sacrificing control. I can do anything, I can know anything, and I promise, there is no other way," she said sadly.

"Well, then you do have limits. On your hope. And your imagination." I pulled out the tablet and went to the core settings for the park, tapping in the ultimate reset codes. The system booted up and started the process.

1%

Dooley rushed at me, trying to wrestle the tablet away. It plummeted to the ground, and I kicked it a few feet behind me as we struggled.

4%

I pinned Dooley, but she flipped me over and pinned me down. I heard footsteps approaching. More police, probably.

Great, just great.

I pushed Dooley off me and tried to get to the tablet, but she grabbed my leg.

"Leave! They're coming, Cam! Please, leave! Save yourself!" she begged.

I kept crawling until she pounced on my back. I couldn't move at all now.

"Reset twenty-five percent complete," the tablet announced. Dooley reached out to grab it. She'd deactivate it, probably drag me out of the park, and send me away. I'd never see her again, or my parents, or Rich. It was all over.

"Let us give you a hand with that."

The voice came from behind us. It sent a chill down my spine.

Dooley and I froze, then looked through the foggy atmosphere. Three figures cut through the mist.

I held my breath as they sharpened into view.

Woody, in his heavy boots and flowing white lab coat. He pushed his glasses up on his nose, then crossed his arms and sneered.

My fake mom, standing tall and rigid, her smile too crooked to be genuine. "What are you doing, Cameron?"

My fake dad, hunched over, ready to charge like a raging bull. "This isn't allowed!"

Their eyes glowed red.

Dooley and I looked at one another, then back at our competition.

"Be cool, D," I said. "Be very cool." My stomach squeezed, and a chill shot through me.

"Count on it," Dooley replied.

We charged at the evil revs. Woody grabbed Dooley by her hair and slung her around. I shot toward my fake mom and tried to push her over. My fake dad swiped at me.

I rolled around in the dust to avoid him.

Dooley scrambled to her feet and kicked Woody right in the stomach. He fell backward, and she started to make her way to me. He jumped on her back.

"Dooley!" I shouted.

Dooley and Woody rolled around in the dust. I flattened myself against the ground, protecting the tablet.

"Give that to me," my fake mom screamed, kicking me.

"No!" I screamed. "No!"

The tablet and I went flying a few feet away.

Woody slammed Dooley and charged at me. He grabbed my shirt and lifted me in the air with one hand. My fake mom put the tablet in his other hand.

Dooley ran at him but stopped short.

We all looked at each other, no one moving.

"Put him down!" Dooley yelled at Woody.

"Or *what*?" Woody taunted.

Dooley took two steps toward him, ready to knock him over.

"Not so fast, darling." Another voice came from behind.

Dooley froze.

We turned to find Southmore standing a dozen feet away, surrounded by police and revs. They circled around us in dozens.

"So you've been hiding our hostages, huh?" Southmore asked Dooley. "I saw that little trick the boy pulled up in the Realm of Realities. Clever, I'll give you that much. But I've got some revs headed up there now to take care of them. Play time is over."

"Don't you hurt them!" I shouted.

"Shut up, kid. Woody, bring him over here."

"Reset fifty percent complete," the tablet said.

Both Dooley and I looked back at it. I had almost forgotten it. In a flash, Woody threw the tablet on the ground, raised his heavy lab boot, and crushed the tablet beneath his foot.

"NO!" I screamed. "Dooley, help!"

Dooley jittered, looking around the circle at all the people. She took a deep breath. She swept Woody's legs from under him with a kick.

He fell to the ground and dropped me, too. My

pretend parents moved to grab Dooley, but she grabbed me from behind and put me in a choke hold, still facing Southmore. The circle of revs and police moved to close in, but Southmore stopped them.

"Now, now, let's not be hasty. Go ahead and hand the kid over, and we'll straighten all this out," he ordered Dooley.

"No! I won't let you destroy him. I've seen what you do. I'll destroy him myself. At least it will be painless," she said, her voice panicked.

Southmore chuckled and took a handkerchief out of his pocket, mopping his head with it.

"Silly child, I don't want to destroy the boy. He's made quite a little fuss for me out there." He pointed toward the outside gate of Centennial Olympic Park. "Somebody's butler is waiting on him, and they'll get mighty suspicious if he doesn't show up. He came with a friend, but that's perfect for our final casualty. Futureland is done. But I need Cameron Walker to step out of here tonight with every hair in place on his pretty little head. My plan depends on it."

Dooley spun around. She kept her grip tight on my throat.

I thrashed and kicked but couldn't free myself. I squeaked out her name.

Southmore smiled patiently, waiting for her to follow orders.

"Well, darling, I'm waiting. All that extra Reasoning I gave you sure is slowing down your response time. I suppose that won't matter soon, anyway. . . ."

"I'll still destroy him! I'll do it right now! Stay back."

Southmore's expression hardened. "Look, no more games. You wouldn't hurt Cam, now, would you? Your first friend? Your very best friend in the world? Hand him over. Don't mess this up for me."

"No! Let us leave or I'll destroy him. Let me get him out of here to safety. He'll never come back. You can do whatever you want with me after. I promise."

"I don't take promises from machines," Southmore said coldly. "You're nothing more than an oversized computer. You really think you can get out of here?! You're surrounded. There's no way you can escape. I've been asking nicely, but don't make me do this the hard way. You know how that feels."

Dooley stood still.

"Fine. Take her," Southmore said to his henchmen.

The crowd started to close in from all sides, my pretend parents and Woody leading the way. Dooley shuffled around, but it was impossible to keep her eyes on the entire crowd. They drew in closer to us, and she whimpered softly.

I'm sorry, Cam. I love you.

I heard her voice in my head. Her grip on my throat tightened even more. The circle of revs closed in. I felt them pulling at my arms and legs and trying to rip Dooley away from me.

Wait.

That was it!

"Dooley," I gurgled, her grip still tight on my neck. "This isn't over."

How, Cam?

I concentrated super hard and remembered all the times I'd heard Southmore speak. In the condo, in the warehouse, and here in the park. And then I focused on one tiny phrase I'd heard him say. I whispered, doing my best Southmore imitation, with my last bit of breath.

"Voice recognition, Blaise. Command Mode."

Dooley winced, her body convulsing against mine as she held me. *Code word required,* I heard in my mind.

"Martha. Resume total park reset. Save—save Futureland."

Dooley and I were on the ground now, surrounded by revs jabbing at us with their makeshift weapons and pulling her from all sides, trying to deconstruct her. Then I heard:

Resuming from fifty percent . . .

With my last burst of energy, I sprang up and kicked a couple of revs. I climbed over Dooley's body, pushing revs to the side. I thrashed and kicked and punched. But I couldn't fight them all.

Reset seventy-five percent complete . . .

One rev kicked me off Dooley. I rolled over on my side, wind knocked out of me. He planted his foot on my chest. I struggled to breathe. My vision turned fuzzy, and my body tired.

What was I going to do? How could I fix this?

A harsh light shone from above. I shielded my eyes. The revs' grips on me loosened, then released me. The destinies started to rotate. The Millennium Marketplace resumed, its band music carrying through the night. The bioluminescent plants glowed in the dark.

Ultimate reset complete.

THE ATLANTA DIARY DECLARATION

Atlanta's Premier Daily News Source

#MISSINGKIDSMARCH ACTIVIST
FINDS MISSING KIDS, SAVES FUTURELAND

September 27, 2048

The only thing more amazing than the Futureland park is the series of events that have unfolded there during the last month.

Friday night, Iman Sheffield and "Juju"

Julien, both missing for weeks, were found *inside* the Futureland park after several kids, including park heir Cameron J. Walker, snuck in after hours to find them. Park founders Dr. Stacy and J. B. Walker were also found captive in the park. When asked what spurred the decision to search within the park itself, Cam Walker simply replied, "Intuition." He will be honored next week at the capitol building for his amazing detective work.

Much of the Futureland hacking was linked to the Atlanta Disuse and Redevelopment Corporation, seemingly in an effort to gain control over the park's patents and technology for financial gain. Police are still searching for Blaise Southmore, CEO of ADRC, who has been missing since last night.

We're not sure what's next for Futureland, but even amid the whirlwind of confusion, a great tragedy has ended, and a great evil has been halted, at least for the moment. When the *ATL Diary Declaration* asked Cam Walker how one kid could

CONTINUED ON NEXT PAGE

make such a big differ-
ence, he insisted:

"It wasn't just one kid.
I couldn't have done it without my friends. We
did it together. We found
Juju and Iman. We saved
Futureland."

**ASHLEY GRAHAM, WITH CONTRIBUTING WRITERS
COOP COOPER AND THAÌS CADIEUX**

Culture Correspondent & Digital Producer

Dear friends, family, guests, and visitors:

We're writing to apologize to you.

   We came to Atlanta because it is home. We wanted to share the magic of the worlds we've created with you. We wanted you to dream, imagine. We wanted you to feel limitless. We never imagined things would happen this way, and we will always hold some pain in our hearts that our dear Futureland was the site of so much fear, confusion, and hurt during our return.

   But we will make things right.

   And we will be back.

   We appreciate all the letters of support and offers to volunteer in the park as we reset our codes, service our revs, and undo many, many terrible things that have been done. Give us a little more time. We're almost there. See you in the Future.

                 The Walkers

23

SOMETHING NORMAL

Sunday, December 20, 2048
10:45 a.m.

"There he is, my right-hand man." Uncle Trey stepped into the doorway of my bedroom, smiling softly. His hair had grown a lot while Southmore held him captive in the same warehouse Rich and I had spied on. Some vacation. And he definitely hadn't cut it since his release from jail. He was sporting a mini-fro and a beard that was slowly filling in. *Makes me look rugged,* he said. "Big day today. You coming out for it? . . . Only if you're up to it," he added. "You can't rush these things, you know."

I closed the photo album in my lap and took a deep breath. "Yeah, I know, Unc. I think I'm feeling up to it. I'll be out in a second."

"Breakfast is ready when you are."

After he left, I opened the album one more time. I stared down at a photo of Dooley and me, not much different from every other one in the album, except this one was the first one we ever took together. I remembered the day—my parents had just finished recoding her. We eyed each other up and down, taking in all the similarities.

Then we played chess.

Dooley beat me three times in a row. Mom and Dad came back into my room to us laughing and playing and snapped this picture—the two of us sitting on the bed, grinning ear to ear, me holding up bunny ears behind Dooley's head.

I swallowed the lump in my throat. What happened a couple of months ago barreled into my head. I couldn't stop seeing Southmore's face. He hacked Mom and Dad's Futureland code and programmed the revs to create chaos and danger inside the park. He wanted to make it unsafe, to get it condemned by the city so that he could take control of it. And use the revs and the technology to create a Future City—like the one my dad once dreamed of. But a real version, in Atlanta.

The memories of it make me so mad. I traced my finger over Dooley's face in the photo. Her smile. She saved us all, ruining his plan. The more I think about that night, and our first night playing chess, I realize that though he may have changed the way hundreds of revs operated, Southmore had nothing to do with Dooley. She was always more than just a rev. She was always limitless.

She always will be.

I blinked away tears.

"We can't save her, Cameron," my dad had said a few days ago, his eyes as teary as mine.

The mayor's office had sent our family an apology and a pardon, but not without their own terms. They demanded that we deprogram and recode every rev involved in the Futureland mystery before the park could open to the public again. In the weeks after, my parents' and Uncle Trey's memories had come back, along with Iman's and Juju's. Even though Dooley had been under the partial control of Southmore, they all remembered *her* as the one who had first snatched them. I pleaded with my parents to find another way. I begged and cried. But there was nothing they could do.

"She's badly corrupted," Mom said, analyzing the data from Dooley's brain chip on the computer in her lab. "Whatever he did with her code, she was trying to fight it. And she did an amazing job. There were only certain ways he could control her. Most times, she was only halfway following commands—finding loopholes. She had started to interpret instructions through her own knowledge and make her own decisions about what to do. That's why she hid us in the Hourglass House instead of 'disposing' of us like he told her to."

"But, Mom, that's—that's—"

"I know, Cam-Cam. It's autonomy. It's evolution. It's an old theory from our early days that we thought was impossible. How a rev could reach independence—humanness—through a series of their own experiences. How an omni-rev could be born."

"There are gaps in her programming that we can't patch up. We'll never be able to control her again. You know as well as we know, Big Man, predictability means safety. If we can't make things right with the City of Atlanta, it may be the end of us," Dad said. "We have to do what they say."

I lost my best friend.

She gave herself up, for me. For us. For Futureland. She saved our world.

I took a deep breath and wiped the tears from my cheeks. I closed the photo album, then tiptoed out of my bedroom to find Uncle Trey sitting at the breakfast bar. He had his mouth covered, giggling. We met eyes, and he motioned for me to get a load of Grandma Ava over the stove, edging Alejandro out of the way while Aurielle stood to the side.

"Maybe you can learn a bit better than that gal over there. She sweet as cherry pie and can clean a kitchen like nobody's business, but she ain't no cook if I do say so myself. Now, let me tell you like I told her—these here is called *grits*—and you got to stir them with love. Can't let them get lumpy. Keep them moving!"

"Abuelita Ava," Alejandro protested. "Give me back the spoon. I've never heard of such a dish."

"That's Grandma Ava to you, young man," she replied. "And that's 'cause you ain't from the South!" She kept her elbow and wrist working double time in the pot.

"Good morning, y'all. Seen my parents?" I interrupted.

Grandma Ava whipped around, then shoved the spoon back into Alejandro's chest and hustled over. She hugged me so tight, I couldn't tell which one would suffocate me first—her squeeze or her perfume.

"My sweet grandbaby. You don't have to go into the park today if you're not ready. I talked to your parents good and long about that—and they understand. That's why I'm here today. I came to protect my baby! And to fix him some breakfast."

A grease pop sounded off from the stove, and a flame rose out of the pot all the way to the exhaust fan.

Alejandro and Aurielle jumped back. Grandma Ava put one hand on her hip and the other on her forehead.

"It's okay, Grandma. I'm ready. And it's almost time. How about some granola for now?" I smiled at her.

I took the elevator to the Guest Hub platform. My stomach felt like it was taking an elevator up to my throat. The ride up to the park would never feel the same as before.

I guess today *was* different. Special. And I was different, too. A lot had changed since we first came to Atlanta.

The doors opened. My parents wore Santa hats and stood surrounded by winter holograms and decorations. Mini candy canes and jingle bells danced in the overhead space, and four Christmas trees, one in each corner, framed the room. Tables held gifts, boxes, kinaras, menorahs, and snacks.

My parents hugged me. I pulled my deerstalker out of my pack pocket and pulled it on.

"Nice touch, kid," Dad said. "And the new suit fits." He smoothed the top of my new Futureland jumpsuit—triple black from head to toe, except for a smooth streak of shimmering hazel running from left shoulder to right hip. And right above the Futureland symbol on the left lapel was a new tiny icon: a tiny, circular brown face, featureless except for two outlined circles atop the head—two afro-puffs.

"You ready?" Mom said.

I took a deep breath. "Ready."

Dad strapped on his cordless mic. "It is our honor to be back, with your help, doing what we love and what we do best. You all know the amazing story of how our son, Cameron Walker, kept this park from ruin and rid Atlanta of an even greater evil. You've celebrated him with letters, calls, and posts on social media. But today, we celebrate his way—in the way that means the most to him. By honoring his friends with our first annual Dooley Day extravaganza. Now, we'd like to open this special day by admitting our first two honored guests. . . ."

I walked over to the platform and triggered the automatic doors. Iman Sheffield and Juju Julien came in with their families. We fitted them for Futureland gear and gave them Futurewatches and lifetime Future Passes.

The crowd cheered. Visitors came in group by

group, and their chosen park destinies rotated to meet them.

My mind raced as I watched them enjoy the park.

"This is the weirdest and coolest thing to ever happen to me," Iman said. "I never want to leave this place. I never want to be normal again."

Normal.

A word I wanted to be for so long.

But seems like the harder I tried to be normal, the weirder my life got.

My parents would always be in the news, and I guess everyone at school would always know my name . . . but I had all a kid could want. What was there to complain about?

I smiled at guests and scanned their Future Passes as they passed through.

I'd never take it for granted again.

An alert buzzed on my Futurewatch.

Angel, Earl, Rich, and Yusuf's little faces danced around one another like a carousel on the hologram projection. I opened up the message.

"Hey, y'all. What's up?"

"Ayo! Cameron Juanita Walker!" Rich shouted.

I chuckled. "What's up, man?"

"What you doing?" Angel asked. "You at the park?"

"Yeah," I whispered. "It's Dooley Day."

"Happy Dooley Day," they all said, almost in unison.

"That's all well and good," Earl said. "But are you coming outside?"

"Outside? What do you mean?"

"Oh, oh. Big man Cam, detective hero, now he don't know what outside is anymore." Rich rolled his eyes.

A rock bounced off the exterior pane of the Futureland entrance platform. The guests inside froze. I walked over to the window and looked out.

There they were. All my new friends, dressed in warm hats and coats, with their bicycles.

"You goofball. You think we forgot your birthday?" Earl announced.

My heart pounded fast. "I . . . I . . ."

"It's your day!" Yusuf said.

"We could go for hot chocolate," Earl said. I could see him blowing on his hands through the window.

"Or we could go listen to the Christmas carolers." Angel sang her own tune, twirling around. "Or ice-skating."

"We could . . . um . . . we could . . . I don't know, man," Rich said. "We could ride around and knock stuff over. Play, laugh, get into trouble. You know, something normal."

I turned to look at all the visitors inside on the

platform. They smiled at me. My eyes settled on Mom and Dad. They looked at one another, then back at me.

"What are you looking at us for, Big Man?" Dad asked. "Your friends are waiting." They both smiled.

I ran over and wrapped my arms around both of them.

"I love you, Mom and Dad," I said.

"We love you, too, Cam-Cam. Happy birthday," Mom said.

"And Happy Dooley Day," Dad added.

Thunk!

Another rock thudded against the window. I heard Rich's voice from below.

"This boy save one little old world-famous park and now he take forever to get ready! Acting brand-new."

"Those kids better stop throwing rocks, I know that." Mom shook her finger at them, then cracked a smile.

I laughed, pulled my deerstalker down, and bolted to the condo to get some granola for the road. And my bike. And my Future-vision goggles.

Hey, you never know.

And that's what it feels like to live on top of the world.

Well . . . more like above it, if I'm being precise.

MAINTENANCE REPORT
Abrams, Trey
12/21/2048
8:05 a.m.

PARK RESET OUTCOMES

As of today, the major issues caused by the ADRC hacking have been resolved. The park's standard safety and operating settings have been restored.

A total of five custom revs in the likeness of prominent Atlanta figures were found and destroyed, including the Atlanta mayor, the chief of police, and Georgia's own governor.

All revs involved in the hack have been decommissioned, except for one:

Woody the lab assistant—location: unknown.

Woody's tracking bug has been removed. It is only logical to believe that Woody's code and programming may still be corrupted from the hacking. He could pose a threat to anyone he comes into contact with.

RECOMMENDATION:
   Locate Woody immediately and schedule for decommissioning.

METHOD:
   To be decided.

Walkers

You think this is over . . .
But it's just the beginning.
We aren't done with you.
Southmore was only one piece of the
   puzzle. A very small piece.
We will come for you. In fact, we
   already have one of your own on
   our side.
We are many.
We are everywhere.
We are . . . limitless.

THE ARCHITECTS

CAM'S GUIDE TO THE PARK

So, you wanna know how to make your way around Futureland and have the most fun? Well, you came to the right place. I've been keeping this place "kid-approved" since . . . hmm . . . since I learned how to spell *approved*!

BEFORE YOU GO

Futureland is huge! So you're gonna want to wear some comfy shoes. Sure, the Jet-Blur pods will zip you across the park skies wherever you want to go, but personally, my favorite way to explore Futureland is on foot. You get to see much more. Speaking of, make sure you bring your phone, your camera—stuff like that. Futureland is one of a kind—the pictures and video you'll be able to get inside the park are top-quality content. There are streamers who have entire channels dedicated to Futureland!

GETTING INSIDE FUTURELAND

First things first: you have to get *into* the park. And there's no cooler way to arrive in style than by floating up to the entrance in our antigravity beam. It's basically like a warm green light that picks you up off the ground and makes you feel like you're flying. You'll get so high in the air that you'll be able to see the whole city! But don't worry—if you're scared of heights, you can always take the stairs.

BY ANY DREAMS NECESSARY

You *have* to experience these things on your first visit.

#1 Bright Futures: How could I *not* mention Bright Futures, our newest and coolest destiny? Bright Futures will take your deepest desires and turn them into reality. Whether your dream is to become the next president or to win gold in Olympic snowboarding, Bright Futures can help you bring it to life (virtually, of course). My parents like to keep the attractions in the park fresh, so I recommend getting to this one before it's gone!

#2 Future Falls and the Future Ring: Everybody loves our nature-based destinies, but here's some insider advice if you want to have real fun: Head over to Future Falls and the Future Ring. Take a tube around the ring with a couple of buddies. Or splash-dive from the top of the waterfall if you're brave!

#3 Snacks! After all that adventuring, you'll probably need some refreshments. Stop by one of the vendor stands in the park (they're everywhere, you can't miss 'em) and grab a chocolate sky—a Futureland-shaped block of pure milk chocolate—and my favorite drink, a fizzy flow. It's like a bubbly tropical explosion. Top-secret recipe, of course.

#4 The Millennium Marketplace: On your way out, you'll probably want to get something to remember us by. A T-shirt? A supercool postcard? A mug with Dooley's face on it? You'll have to catch the Millennium Marketplace before it zips away. Just keep an eye out for the shimmering silver pop-up shop with jazzy electronic music playing, or ask one of the revs where you can find it.

LAST BUT NOT LEAST

Futureland would be nothing without the cities that invite us to visit. I've been all around the world, and it's taught me that no amount of fancy-schmancy scientific wonder can measure up to the good vibes of making a new friend. Atlanta is a pretty cool city.

Whether you take a ride on the SkyView Ferris wheel or dash into any of the several museums downtown, there's so much to do and enjoy. My uncle Trey always reminds me that *the people make the place,* not the other way around. Remember to dream—but remember to live in the moment, too.

Your friend,
CJ

ACKNOWLEDGMENTS

First and foremost, a tremendous thanks to Dhonielle Clayton and Cake Creative, the originators of this project, for offering me the opportunity to work on it and ushering me through the entire process. For launching my career. For reaching back and pulling our people along, always.

Thanks to Lamar Giles for being a great mentor and for linking me up with D.

Big thanks to Futureland's editor, Tricia Lin, for being a champion of this project and all you did to bring it into the world. Thanks to Jen Valero and April Ward from art and design for their work. Thank you to Diane João and Barbara Bakowski for the stellar copyediting and proofreading. And thanks to the many Random House teams that contributed to make Futureland a reality.

Major thanks to Suzie Townsend, the maestro on the agency side, for juggling more than I can imagine.

Thank you to the entire New Leaf Literary & Media and Cake Creative teams for keeping the wheels turning on this project and maintaining the energy through the finish line.

Thanks to everybody else I'm not even aware of who had a place in creating this art.

Thank you, Khadijah Khatib, for the miraculous cover and illustrations. I'm so glad you chose us.

Thanks to my agent, Leah Pierre of Ladderbird Literary Agency, for supporting me as I work on Futureland. For treating my involvement in this project like it's your own, even though there's no obligation to do so.

Much love to all my friends (new and old), family, and writing community members who have supported me through this entire journey. The fun moments and the tough ones. Many of you were happy for me before you even knew what to be happy for. Thank you for staying down. It means everything.

Sending love, peace, and light to the families of the victims on "The List" from the late seventies and early eighties in Atlanta. Those whose names we know and those names we don't. Thank you for allowing me to amplify your stories and speak power through the names of your angels. Your families deserved better. Your babies deserved better. We won't forget them.

307

Thanks, Rob. I love you, man. I miss you. Wherever you are, I hope it's easy there.

And to the kiddos. The students. The babies. The next generation. Our greatest hope. Y'all are the reason I do it all. Thank you for everything, always.